THE WAY BEYOND

*The Life and Times of
Halycon Sage*

Praise for *The Life and Times of Halycon Sage*

Firstst Edition

Now revised and retitled ***The Way Beyond***

So tightly wrapped and profoundly structured that I'm sure I missed at least 14 significant clues as to the REAL meaning of the narrative!"

—Lennie Major

[D]eliciously funny fiction . . . The tale is a clever, wild mixture of lowbrow and pop-cultural humor . . . weaving a variety of outlandish personalities and points of view into an entertaining, fast-moving novel that is nearly guaranteed to provoke laughter.

—Peter Dabbene
Forward Reviews

It's a madcap novel, leaping and lurching with a frenetic energy reminiscent of mid-1960s postmodernism. The satire is broad . . . yet charming; the silliness is infectious, and Bushnell never pauses in any one place long enough for boredom to set in. Bushnell is an undeniable writer, with a talent for sentences and scenarios."

—Kirkus Reviews

. . . the stirring immediacy of a guitar riff.

—BlueInk Review

THE WAY BEYOND

THE LIFE AND TIMES OF HALYCON SAGE

Karima Vargas Bushnell

Delirious Walrus
Minneapolis, Minnesota, USA

The Sage Chronicles

The Way Beyond:
The Life and Times of Halycon Sage

by Karima Vargas Bushnell

Published by Delirious Walrus Productions LLC
Minneapolis MN

Because of the dynamic nature of the internet, any web addresses or links
contained in this book may have changed since publication
and may no longer be valid.

Paperback: 978-1-7334288-4-2
Ebook: 978-1-7334288-7-3

Library of Congress Control Number: 2023946488

Cover Design by
Richard Ljoenes LLC

Layout and Interior Design by
B.C. Hatch
Into a Book

Edited by
Delirious Walrus Editing Department
Chandi Lyn
B.C. Hatch

Printed in the USA

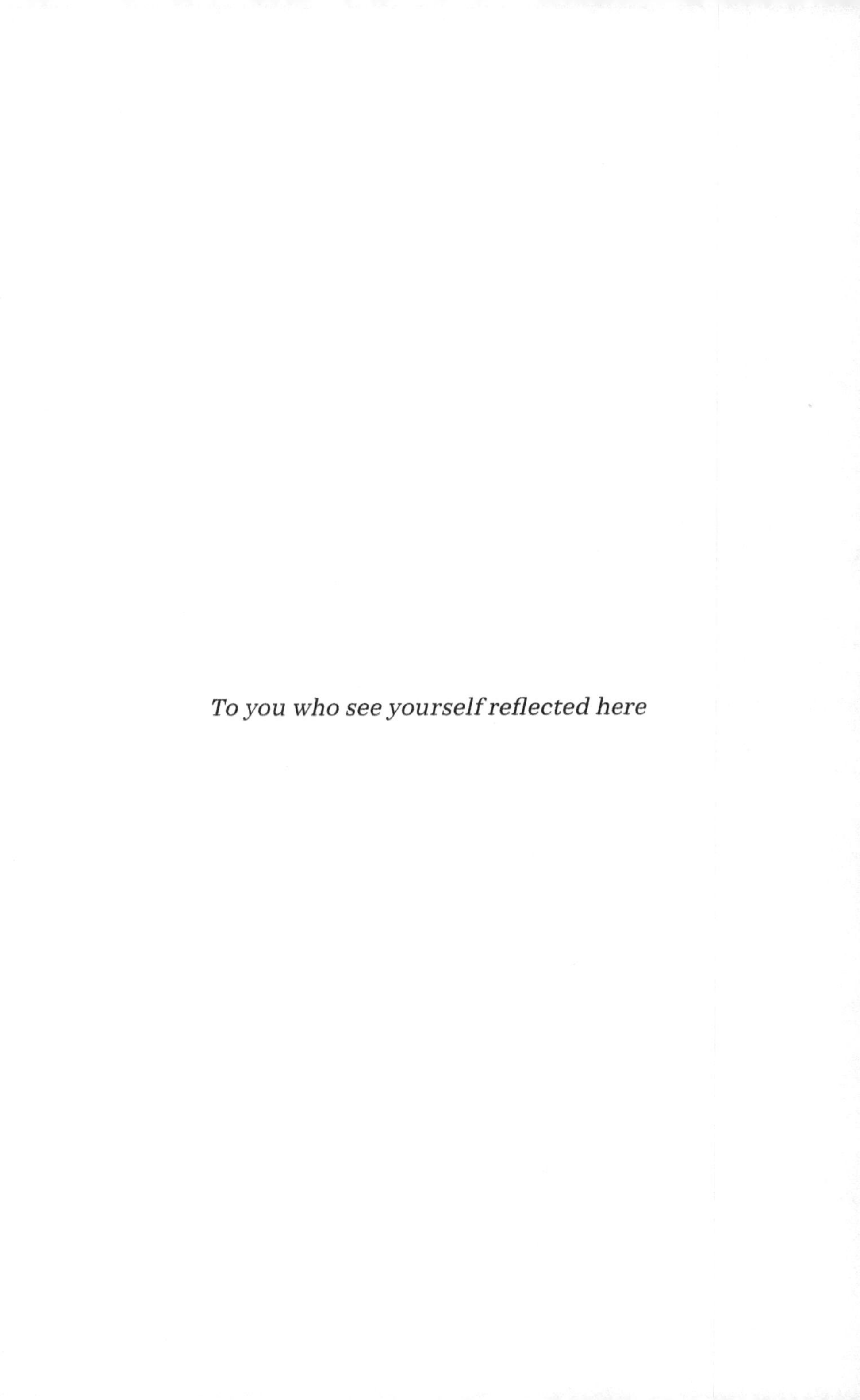

To you who see yourself reflected here

PREFACE TO THE
THIRD EDITION

T HE FIRST ROUGH version of this book was begun around 2003, put aside for years, then finished in two days in 2011 when the demands of work and family life had eased. But life between then and now has changed beyond recognition.

The time is long past when plane travel could be pleasant, not everyone had cell phones and laptops, and a boy could surf questionable content at the public library. The great tsunami and nuclear meltdown of 2011 are history, not current events. Mentions of the Tea Party, internet cafes, and people who wouldn't know a guy named Muhammad was Muslim seem outdated to the point of quaintness. And references to cultures, conditions, and ethnicities in all their richness and beauty are not treated in this book with the finicky niceness required by 2020s standards.

This is a book of its time, and updating these things would do it violence. Indeed, some of these anachronisms are woven inextricably into the fabric of the story. Alexander Preisczech wouldn't have been so sure he was being spied upon without a certain once inescapable but now rare supermarket announcement. The false assumption that this story takes place in today's world could cause you, the reader, to doubt the book's veracity, which would be a shocking thing!

The most obvious change is the new title, *The Way Beyond*, which can be taken in two ways: as either *the way which leads beyond* or as *that which is way beyond* what is normal or expected. Our series embodies both these concepts, beginning with relatively ordinary events and opening out into a new place of multiple meanings, multiple possibilities, and multiple points of view.

May the Horse be with you.

As I write this in October of 2023, life has again changed beyond recognition; the heartbreaking situation exploding in Israel/Palestine came about as we were going to press. While the agony there reaches back to the post-war years, until recently it was largely ignored by those outside the region.

A glancing reference is made to this 'Middle East situation' at the beginning of Chapter Five; the protagonist's earnest but unsuccessful attempts to understand reflect my own, abandoned by the time of writing in 2003.

PROLOGUE

"WHAT'S THIS?" ASKED the Eminence in disbelief. "It reads like nonsense. Random. Aimless . . . "

"It's the forerunner," replied the Squid a little nervously. "The prequel to the Earth-Book that describes the Splitting of Reality, the creation of the Alternate Universe, and all the rest of it. We Squidren played our part," he added modestly.

"Meandering," continued the Eminence, following his own train of thought. He was pleased to have nailed down precisely what bothered him about the first pages of the volume floating before him.

"It's Stream of Consciousness. Like James Joyce," said the Squid reverently. While he knew nothing of James Joyce, he understood that this was a great Earthean figure whose status demanded proper respect.

"James *Bullfeathers*," rumbled the Eminence, who was not constrained by the Squidish notions of manners.

"You have to hang with it a while," continued the Squid,

using an Earth idiom. "It all comes together."

"I should certainly hope so," concluded the Eminence, his enormous flippers waving gracefully. "That will be all."

But it was *not* all. It was barely the beginning.

Dear Editor,

As the only person with positive knowledge of the real identity of the great Sage, I feel it is my duty to forward you this manuscript, part of which was discovered shortly after his disappearance. I hope it reaches you.

It is my hope that in sending this I am doing something for the world, though strictly speaking, the world as we knew it has ended. I know that, as his editor, you think you know who Halycon Sage is (or was). But you don't. You really, really don't.

Yours truly,

R. Elizabeth Echevarria

Disclaimers

Apart from the exceptions given in the Afterword, no person living, dead, supernaturally ascended or cryogenically frozen is real, and any resemblance to actual people is purely coincidental.

No moose were harmed in the writing of this book. References to "mooseheads" are purely literary or autobiographical and in no way intended to incite violence against moosekind.

THE WAY BEYOND

THE LIFE AND TIMES OF HALYCON SAGE

Karima Vargas Bushnell

Delirious Walrus
Minneapolis, Minnesota, USA

CHAPTER
ONE

**ALYCON SAGE WAS** drinking again. He sat in the red leather, no-moosehead bar and pounded them down. He had been like this ever since the publication of his second novel, *Everything in the Universe is Fine Right Now*, and its scathing reception by the critics. The novel in its entirety consisted of one sentence:

But those Indian sports-team names
have got to go!

The negative reaction had come as a complete shock, because his first book had been a stunning, earth-shattering success.

As it is also extremely short, we are reprinting it here:

One Hundred and One Cows: A Novel
by Halycon Sage

There are no cows in this book. What there is, however, is the story of Rory McPhooey, who sailed from the fog-bound coasts of Ireland all by himself in a tiny, tiny boat, all the way to the shores of the Native Americans, who turned him right back around and sent him home again.

The End

Author's Note: This is the story of the European conquests as they might have been. No disrespect is intended to the Irish, who are my very favorite people, except for the Native Americans.

Hamden McPete, a man of courtly demeanor and undoubted scholarship, wrote in his popular column a gentle suggestion that Halycon Sage was overrated. In fact, he declared, Halycon Sage was not only *not* the greatest novelist of our time, he was not a novelist at all. He was not even a no-*vell*-ist, that is, the author of one or more novellas. Sage's works were, in a word, too short. (Well, in two words.)

On the 25th of May, the literati rustled their newspapers over their morning juice in shock. McPete had written, "This creation could be called a Caprice, a Whimsy, or even possibly a Lowland Fling, but it is definitely *not* a novel."

After reading this missive (yes, we know a newspaper column is not a "missive," but it *sounds* right. Listen to the flow of the words—it sings.) After READ-ing this MIS-sive, Halycon Sage stayed drunk for three days. It struck to the very core of his identity. If he was not a novelist, then what was he? An exile from the reservation who could never return? An alien caught in the net of terrifying banality that was that was post-modern civilization? (Halycon Sage was an admirer of Huston Smith's *Beyond the Post-Modern Mind*, and had considered writing a spin-off about developments even more subsequent, titled *Beyond Beyond the Post-Post-Modern Mind*, but his editors had talked him out of it, fearing lawsuits.)

But again, who was he? A lonely hero, anachronistic survivor of the deserts and plains? A man who, instead of running down the enemy on a galloping horse, was struggling to fill out Form 154B, and nearly succumbing to despair over the pink bit at the end? A fireman at the scene of a flood, a man with all the wrong tools, a genius born too early, or too late?

"Oh, God!" his soul cried out from the very depths of his bowels. "Oh, the pain! The lonely, lonely pain!"

Sage stared moodily into his glass, considering for about the 44th time the negative review penned by McPete, kindest of the critics, a man known for his insightful brilliance. The elegant disquisition subtitled, "Could Halycon Sage *himself* be Native American?" continued past the hurtful comment about length to a conclusion that could be summed up more colloquially as, "Nah, he's just a wannabe." The final sentence was unequivocal. "Whatever else he may be, Halycon Sage is *not* a Native American."

I am so, thought Halycon Sage, as he knocked back another one.

INDEED, THE CRITICS were having a lot of fun trying to figure out who or what Halycon Sage actually was. Besides the Native American theory, they thought he was:

- a Somali from Kenya
- an amateur religious scholar with insomnia
- a woman

None of these was correct. Halycon Sage couldn't tell a *Majratan* from an *Ogaden*, didn't know *Advaita* from *Tauheed*, and had never been exasperated by male privilege or had trouble picking out a lipstick.

If they knew his real identity, they would die laughing, but Halycon Sage was keeping the laugh to himself. Nobody knew.

KATHRYN MCCREADY, SAGE'S editor, was the only person who almost knew his identity. She had become concerned that Sage had tipped his hand too much by writing *two* novels with Native themes. By now, the public would be virtually certain he was a Native American male. So, using a variety of pseudonyms, she wrote several short opinion pieces to be strategically placed in magazines and newspapers in the United States and elsewhere. The resulting collection of spin, counter spin, and counter-counter spin created a violent commotion as his aficionados and the literary critics stumbled upon them or hunted them down like detectives, collected them like priceless treasure, and fought over them like buzzards trying to divide a mouse. The editor didn't necessarily want to *lie* to anybody, but she wanted to muddy the waters a little and maintain his mystique. (Halycon Sage himself didn't give a rat's patootie about his mystique.)

These are the things she wrote:

- It is possible that Halycon Sage is some sort of disgruntled religious functionary who feels trapped. The profession and promotion of his religion have become, not only his livelihood, but also his identity. To say—almost to think—anything in conflict with the basic tenets of his faith would violate everything he's been saying and doing for years. Besides, it would disappoint all his friends. One day it occurred to him that all he needed was a new identity. Then he could say and think what he damned well pleased. Thus, Halycon Sage was born.

- Halycon Sage had been stunned to discover that people thought he was Native American, but he realized upon deeper reflection that this might have been expected. The confusion had been going on since 1492, and it wasn't surprising that one lonely wanderer, one vagabond of the spirit, had also been caught up in it. '*Om namo, bhagavate vasudevaya*,' he sang gently to himself as he prepared his meditation seat, already feeling the world-saving calm washing over his mind. 'Oh well, that's the way it goes,' he murmured in his lilting voice, giving the little sideways head-shrug so characteristic of his people.

- With determined stride, Halycon Sage moved along the path beside the little river, her head up, her eyes clear. Only God knew where she was going—even she didn't know—but she would get there in her own way, at her own speed (usually rather fast). Her long hair flowed out behind her, and her beautiful face was carved with the lines of her experience. Halycon Sage was a woman who had suffered, yes, but Halycon Sage was a woman who had *lived*.

The editor herself had been asked many questions about Halycon Sage. She refused to answer them, citing his obsession with privacy, but the truth was that though she had met him, she didn't know who he really was or where he was from or much of anything else about him. Asking him directly got her nowhere, and her subtle and detailed researches had failed as well. She'd never heard of anyone with the first name *Halycon*; it appeared to be merely the misspelling of an adjective. As to his *last* name, the various bits of online trivia, that 3.80 out of 100,000 U.S. Americans were named Sage and so on, were not enormously helpful.

She sighed and went on to more important matters. The editor actually had a theory, but she had never had the nerve to confront him with it. Maybe someday he would tell her.

Mysterious Note

So, where *is* Sage, anyway? At home? Still in the bar? Does he just wander around the town or city or whatever it is, *thinking* things? The next bit sounds as though he's at home, but I'm sure *I* don't know. For God's sake, sir, give us some context! As one of your Earth-authors so pungently puts it, "Watson, I can't make bricks without clay!" (The telltale references to Earth and Sherlock Holmes might hint at a certain extragalactic origin to this note, but best not to speculate; we will say, with its author, that we're sure *we* don't know.)

THE ENIGMATIC AUTHOR drifted off again, as was his habit, thoughts meandering through space and time, what has been and what has not and what may never be. Truth to tell, he sometimes had little idea which was which, which made doing practical things a bit difficult.

Enough of this! Gathering focus, Halycon Sage reflected on the problem he had with his name—two problems, actually. While staying in New York, he'd picked the penname "Sage" to remind him of the sagebrush that covered the far away desert where he'd been born, but everybody thought it meant "wise." That was the minor problem.

The major problem he had was his *first* name, which he pronounced "HAL-i-con." It meant something like, "The Happy Land of Yesteryear," which seemed appropriate, and he liked it a lot. Only right away, people started saying, "Don't you mean *Hal-sea-on*?" (Sage had probably not sounded out the word when he first encountered it, and of course such laziness leads to all sorts of problems.)

This mangling of his name was a constant annoyance, especially when it happened on television. No, he didn't mean Hal-sea-on, which sounded stupid. So, he evolved a method for dealing with it. When interviewers asked, "Don't you mean *Hal-sea-on*?" he simply sat in silence for a long, uncomfortable minute of dead air, then said, "No." That usually ended it. He stopped talking about "The Happy Land of Yesteryear," though. It was gone anyway.

But he still remembered the smell of sage in the rain. It was rare and precious and permeated everything. Unlike the sage smell, which still appeared on uncommon rainy occasions in the western states, the tumbleweeds seemed to be gone completely, as if they had never existed. There's nothing like the sight of three or four tumbleweeds somersaulting down the street, the dusty wind making little snapping noises in your ears like sheets flapping on a laundry line. Maybe they had all rolled off to the Happy Land of Tumbleweeds or something. Halycon Sage had once hacked through a forest of compacted tumbleweeds, blown together into a clump that ran for miles. He thought he'd give The Happy Land of Tumbleweeds a miss.

As his thoughts turned to his first serious attempt to write a real novel—well, his autobiography anyway—he realized that he had *another* problem. If people mangled his name when they interviewed him on television, then his identity couldn't be secret. It had to be one or the other. (The way his thoughts unspooled through time and space, looping and turning, it was not entirely unusual for him to face alternate realities even in daily life.)

Some writers might have given up at this point, but Halycon Sage was used to the inconsistency of the universe— he'd been fighting it for decades—or a shorter period if, as some suggested, he was actually an alienated teenager.

Putting the problem aside for the moment, he raised his pen and wrote:

**The Crushing Fall and Phoenix-Like
Resurgence of Halycon Sage:
Part Forty-Two of The Chronicle of My Life:
Stuff I Did, Why I Did It, What It Felt Like,
and Why You Should Care.**

The characters in what you are about to read are fictional, and any resemblance to real people living, dead, supernaturally ascended, or cryogenically frozen, is purely coincidental . . .

And then he was stuck. Moodily he considered just forgetting the whole thing and heading for the wide-open spaces.

WAKING UP WITH one of those attacks of brilliance that sometimes come during sleep, Halycon Sage found the solution to his problem about remaining anonymous while simultaneously meeting strangers who mispronounced his name. He had thought he would have to resort to alternate time tracks, but it was much simpler than that. He only gave *radio* interviews.

His eccentric desire never to be identified bordered on mania. During interviews, he habitually spoke through one of those voice distorters that witness protection programs use. Linguists had analyzed his sentence structure and word choice, but since these changed with his mood, it hadn't gotten them anywhere. And he had twice appeared on television, but *appeared* is not exactly the right word. He'd arrived wearing a huge black contraption of his own devising, like the Afghani burka but draped over a light wire frame, effectively concealing everything about him.

His disguise made Halycon Sage look like the Elephant in the Living Room, tastefully draped in black. In fact, Halycon

Sage *was* the Elephant in the Living Room. Well, no, he thought, laying down his pen. That's not the right idiom. The joker in the deck, the wildcard in an otherwise orderly universe? But the universe *wasn't* orderly, and those images had implications of mischief and troublemaking that he didn't want. *I'm Chaotic Good*, thought Sage, who'd played a bit of Dungeons and Dragons in his time. And he floated off into a glassy-eyed writer's daze of speculation, further postponing the accomplishing of any meaningful work.

HALYCON SAGE WAS saved by Basel Vasselschnauzer, another influential critic who responded like an attack badger on May 26th in his own equally popular column, "What We Like and Why."

"Professor McPete," he wrote, "has lain too long on the couch of complacency, beneath the closed and curtained window of tradition, within the ivory towers of academe . . ." "*Ack-add-deem,*" he said under his breath. "*Ack-cad-dee-mee. Ack-a-day-mee-yah.*" Deciding that he only had to *write* his column, not read it aloud to anybody, he continued. His overweening arrogance and the conviction that he was the busiest man on earth precluded any consulting of a dictionary or online source for the correct pronunciation. It never even occurred to him.

"WE LIKE HALYCON SAGE," he wrote, in a stirring whatever the opposite of a denunciation is. "Sage is a true artist, and his genius is his embrace of the minimalist tradition. Sage is the standard bearer for all that is simple, clean, clear, and yet complex. One word of Sage's is worth a thousand words of lesser authors. I say, 'Hats off to Halycon Sage! Long may he wave!'"

The mention of hats reminded him to add something to the formulaic list of further likes and dislikes he always included at the bottom of his column. "Oh, and WE LIKE THE BERET. They're coming back. I say so."

And so it was that Halycon Sage rose again, inspired by the defense of Basel Vasselschnauzer and the groundswell of support in the best literary circles. And indeed, the furor had far-reaching effects, extending even beyond the bounds of Literature and into Art as a whole, where the New Minimalism of Halycon Sage wrought changes in Painting, Sculpture, Music, Film, and Television. Inspired by his success, an Arabian painter created a huge piece consisting of a dot in the center of an enormous white sheet of canvas, claiming that the dot was "the point beneath the *Bismillah*."[1] (The theological basis of his claim was sound, and the Art Piece sold for ten thousand dollars.)

So Halycon Sage, the luminosity of his name ever increasing, rose and shot across the firmament of human consciousness like a blazing meteor, a fire of truth against the deep blue evening sky, like Herman Hesse, only even better. And he wrote his third novel, the greatest of them all:

> And a man went forth, and he did everything right. But everything went wrong anyway.

> The End

And the Immortals looked down and read what Halycon Sage had written. And they laughed.

BEFORE THIS COMPLETELY unexpected resurgence of his literary career, Halycon Sage had been conducting a marathon-length pouting session. He pouted a lot. Even though he pretended not to care what

---

1. *Bismillah,* meaning, "In the Name of God," begins the first chapter of the *Qur'an,* called the *Fatiha* (the Opening). There is a teaching that esoterically the whole Qur'an is contained in the *Fatiha,* the *Fatiha* in the *Bismillah,* and the *Bismillah* in the dot or point beneath its first letter, *bah.*

Hamden McPete had written about him, he really, really did. He hadn't written a word for weeks and had pined so disconsolately that he was in a fair way to lose the distinctive little potbelly he had acquired through literary success. (Sage was not immediately conscious of the furor caused by Vasselschnauzer's defense; he had sworn off all media as part of his sulks.)

He had enormous respect for McPete, far more than he had for Basel Vasselschnauzer, the critic who had leaped to his defense. McPete was known for his sound scholarship, unerring judgment and quiet good taste, whereas Vasselschnauzer had no judgment at all and formed his passionate attachments and virulent hatreds of authors instantaneously (sometimes without even reading their books) based on whatever would enhance his ego and annoy his friends, enemies, and rivals. McPete heard about Sage's distress and wrote a kindly note of inquiry and good wishes for his health. In response, Sage sat up, opened the curtains, and began to believe that one day he would write again.

CHAPTER
TWO

**HERE WERE DAYS** when Halycon Sage thought a lot of people were fools, but he tried to be nice to them anyway. It gave him indigestion. On the other hand, he was stunned by his own incompetence. With all his advantages, he couldn't do things high school dropouts and one-armed immigrants with Post Traumatic Stress Syndrome did every day, like go out and get a job. His awareness of his incompetence did not give him indigestion, but it made him stare like a rabbit in the headlights, hoping the whole thing would go away.

One day, it did. He *made* everything go away just by leaving, without telling his editor, without telling anyone. He only gave away his goldfish to a neighbor who had no idea he was famous.

"Adios, amigo," said Halycon Sage to the goldfish. With that, he mounted his faithful horse and rode off into the vast reaches of even deeper anonymity.

HALYCON SAGE'S LOYAL mount was a horse with no name, because he loved the song of the same title. The only problem was that there was no way to effectively *call* this horse. So, by a natural process of linguistic development, the horse came to be known as No-Name Stupid, to which he responded readily.

The Horse with No Name thing was kind of like the situation with The Artist Formerly Known as Prince. Remember? The pop star who changed his name to an unpronounceable symbol? It just didn't work out very well in real life.

Halycon Sage loved the song, but one line in it made him laugh himself silly:

"After two days (pause) in the desert sun
My skin began to turn red."

Had the songwriter ever *been* in the desert? The line should have been:

"After two days (pause) in the desert sun
My skin began to resemble charred barbecue."

Perhaps this lonely iconoclast who had turned his back on civilization to seek his soul in the trackless desert put on UV sun block every two hours.

It would have been more consistent with Halycon Sage's mission if he had camped out every night, but he'd given up camping in bad weather since a miserable night in a news-making rainstorm in Klamath Falls, Oregon. Several inches of water had come through the bottom of the tent, and Sage and his friends had eventually decamped to drink coffee in a warm and welcoming diner on a nearby hill. By the time he ran away, Sage's idea of roughing it included a fair number of these little digressions.

His new attention to comfort presented the rather ridiculous problem of sneaking a horse into motel rooms. (Leaving Stupid outside was unthinkable. Besides the lack of hitching posts and the possibility of drawing unwanted attention, they would have missed each other.) After a few weeks of practice, the two developed a reliable system.

Sage would park the horse a few hundred feet away, near a cottonwood tree or a stand of poplars, if possible, where it would wait casually, as if it had some business there. The casualness was a bit too studied. The horse seemed to be waiting for a bus, or about to light a cigarette. But so far no one had complained.

No-Name Stupid was actually very bright. Sage could point to the door of their prospective room and the horse would look at the motel, not at his pointing finger, as animals are reputed to do. Then Sage would go to the office, claim the room he had previously booked, obtain the key, and unlock the door, opening it about a quarter inch. If the room was in sight of the office, he would return to distract the manager with innocent banter about hunting, fishing, road conditions or car repairs. Meanwhile, the horse walked quickly to the room and pushed the door open with his nose, closing it behind him in the same way.

No-Name Stupid watched television, but he did not try to sleep in the bed, which was a *good* thing. He stood quietly in a corner, nibbling on shredded wheat and apples provided for his enjoyment, then slept the sleep of the just—the sleep of a brown and white pinto who knows that his rider is on an exalted mission.

His mission was bigger than 'finding himself,' though that played a part. Quite simply, Halycon Sage was out to save the world. Among his oddly assorted and frequently useless gifts was this: He understood the secrets of the universe. He could see how the whole thing was put together, how every part interacted and why each thing and creature was the way it was. He did not understand this in a physical science kind of way, but he could see the meaning, the patterns, the conflicting and harmonious forces and how they played out in every event.

What bothered him was that there was no way to *explain* it to anybody. He had tried, and tried hard, but since nothing was really separate from anything else—all boundaries were convenient illusions and figures of speech—he always wound up with a pedantic listing or an incoherent babbling. This was why he had resorted to his minimalist novels of one or two sentences. It was neither to be arty or annoying as some people thought, nor because of the focused simplicity of his genius, as was believed by others. It was simply a way he had found of transmitting a tiny bit of what he knew in a way that would not be completely rejected.

This tendency to see everything as connected to everything else led to the third, secret reason he had run away, a secret he kept from everyone, even himself. When he finally headed into the desert, it was not only to save the world, and not only to find himself. He had also run away from the Mail Pile. He thought of it as the Snarl of Inhuman Things, a snarl in the sense of a hopeless tangle, but sometimes also in the sense of an invading hostility within his own home, watching him with fangs bared. It was nothing more than a fairly large pile of the stuff that got delivered every day, and it should have been easy to deal with, but it wasn't.

Letters from actual human beings were not the problem. You could respond to them or throw them away. Pitiful letters from the dozens of charities he had once contributed to could be dealt with likewise. He still cared, of course—about both the causes and the fans—but because it was all just too much, they often found a home in the circular file.

Even the straightforward bills weren't too bad. He could write a check, stick on a stamp, and mail an envelope, an activity that filled him with an absurd sense of triumph and satisfaction. Sometimes he even walked the five blocks to the postal collection box to prolong the feeling, instead of simply sticking the letters in the mailbox outside his door.

The little pile of utility bills in his hand proved that reality was still understandable and that he could prevail over it. Somebody somewhere had generated electricity, or water. Some of this stuff came to his house. He used it, and therefore had to pay for it. He paid for it. A simple exchange of goods and services for legal tender, not too different from exchanging a fish for a string of beads. It was similar to the beauty of the rain cycle, in which water fell down, was used by plants and animals, poured out again, collected in lakes and streams, and eventually evaporated to repeat the process.

No, none of these things bothered him. It was the Others. Things like, "Capital growth five percent investment mortgage devaluation income card statement. Open immediately. Do not discard." How on earth was a man, a living, breathing human being with desires, fears, and morals, likes and dislikes—a body, mind, and spirit— supposed to deal with that? Death could be met with honor, illness with patience, joy with celebration. But what was the proper human response to *this*? There *was* none.

Had there been only one of these enormities, he could have thrown it away, or called someone to find out if he really had to do anything about it. But there wasn't just one. There were hundreds. And because Halycon Sage could never remember which of these nameless, faceless corporations and subsidiaries he actually had dealings with, he had no way to identify the ones that were merely pretending. He might have shipped the whole mess off to his lawyer, but this thought had never occurred to him. Halycon Sage was in some ways a simple soul, and besides, he could never find the lawyer's address.

The most terrifying thing about these letters was that they were written by machines. The signatures at the bottom had never known a human hand or pen, were probably not even facsimiles. They were letters from machines, fit only to be read and answered by machines. There was no person on the other end, anxious or cranky or concerned, awaiting a reply. And the curse of Halycon Sage was that he only cared about human things. Human things and animal things and heavenly things and even hellish things, but not writings generated by machines.

It was like his money. He had no idea how much he had—quite a lot, apparently. But he had been bludgeoned into Direct Deposit by his editors, so he never had the pleasure of an actual check in his hand, convincing him that he had done something worthy of compensation in the real world. And just as the money came in, mysterious and unannounced, so it went out again, through Automatic Withdrawal. There seemed to be no need for any real Halycon Sage to be part of the process, creating novels and using goods and services. He was superfluous.

This was the third, secret reason that Halycon Sage had run away to the desert. He had decided the machines could get on with their work just as well without him.

CHAPTER
THREE

**AVE YOU EVER** tried to navigate the post-modern world on a horse? Halycon Sage was fairly sure horses weren't allowed on the freeway, so he kept to the smaller roads. He also suspected that some places had ordinances about horses on public streets, but since he had no way of knowing what they were, the whole thing was concerning. The local authorities might not know what they were either, but this wouldn't prevent them from making things up. Sage had a hard enough time navigating his inner and outer realities without considering variations among the horse laws of Buckeye, Sawtooth Gap, Imploded Pickle Ridge or whatever the hell else was out there. Possible variations seemed infinite, and fraught with peril.

He had found a way of dealing with Stupid's possible illegality, though he wasn't too proud of himself about it.

When he came into the sort of town a Black friend of his youth had described, running changes on an old commercial, as "the *red-neckiest*," he simply pulled out what was in his right saddlebag and put it on his head. It was a full-out, not-too-cheap fake Indian headdress obtained on sale from a movie studio. Wearing this regalia, Halycon Sage assumed an earnest and proud expression, rode through the town with head held high, and no one ever bothered him. Little kids cheered or laughed, and policemen saluted. They assumed, naturally, that he was the advance guard or tail end of some parade or event they hadn't heard about.

Halycon Sage hoped he never ran into any real Native Americans while he was wearing this getup, because they would have beaten him to a pulp—or worse, laughed till they fell over. Halycon Sage, being possibly of mixed heritage, had a lot of anxiety about whether or not he was a Real Indian. But in spite of his embarrassment, he definitely had to get his horse past the cops, and this worked.

Knowing that Halycon Sage had an enormous, flashy, fake-Indian headdress in his right saddle bag, complete with good-quality simulated eagle feathers, it might be asked what exactly was in his *left* saddle bag. The bag could easily have contained his clothing, sturdy work boots or shiny cowboy boots, canteen, lasso, and other good stuff like that, or even food or blankets.

Unfortunately, it did not. It contained horse manure. Towns and cities had other ordinances, more universal than the ones forbidding horses on the streets. They were pick-up-after-your-pet ordinances. An old lady had once scared the bejeesus out of Halycon Sage by leaning out a window and screaming at him the *one time* he had failed to pick up after his boxer dog. He wasn't about to make the same mistake with a horse, especially since some of the cops were just dying to bust a fake Indian on a brown and white pinto, even one who was trying to save the world.

So, with an absurd headdress in one saddlebag and a load of manure in the other, Halycon Sage went riding, riding, riding. Through desert dawns and silent morning towns, past sparkling watered lawns and beds of brilliant, sun-washed flowers, through rowdy Saturday nights with neon flashing and music blaring. He rode past snowcapped mountains and iconic western wear stores, over big, stony rivers and little gurgling streams, past people and the absence of people, with white sky and blue sky and soaring birds and the smells of pine and sage he loved.

No anxious editor. No mail pile. No adoring fans (since no one could recognize him). And best of all, no Basel Vasselschnauzer.

Ah, thought Halycon Sage, *this is the life.*

CLIP-CLOPPING THROUGH Nevada between Carson City and Reno, Sage was passing by The Hangman ("Lousy Food—Warm Beer"), when he noticed a new place next door. He had always liked The Hangman, which had been there forever, and he had been sorry when they took down the old wooden sign, cracked and peeling though it was.

This new place advertised buffalo burgers, fresh-squeezed orange juice, and homemade pie. At this point in the day, Sage would have eaten a Twinkie and Cheetos sandwich, but this menu looked good. He noted with amusement that there were two ornamental hitching posts outside the entrance and used one of them to tie up No-Name Stupid, then went inside to place his order.

Coming out a few minutes later to give Stupid his Giant Homemade Oatmeal Cookie (All Natural), he saw that a second horse was tethered beside him. This was very unusual. It looked as though he wasn't the only one still using a horse for actual travel.

There was a funny wooden thing on the other horse's back, holding the saddlebags. *What on earth could that be*, he wondered.

Back in the restaurant, Sage sat down next to a young man at the counter, evidently the horse's owner. He was thin and slight, but strong looking, with long brown hair and beard. Oddly, he was wearing sandals instead of cowboy boots.

"Howdy, Stranger," said Sage, getting into his Western role. The man nodded politely, smiling a little.

"That your horse?" Sage asked.

"Yup."

"I don't see too many guys on horses, except on the trails. Use him for traveling, do you? It certainly saves gas money."

"Well, usually I walk," said the man, picking a little piece of dirt off his sandal and depositing it neatly in his napkin, "but right now I've got this horse."

"What's that funny-looking thing on his back?"

"That's my yoke," said the man.

Sage wisely avoided the first comment that came into his mind: *That's a yolk, son.* But the pun on egg yolks stuck in his mind.

"My grandmother was allergic to eggs," he said irrelevantly.

"Doesn't it bother the horse?"

"No, not really," said the man. "My yoke is easy, and my burden is light."

"Oh, that's good," said Sage. *Sounds familiar somehow*, he thought to himself. It gave him a funny feeling.

"So, what brings you here?"

"Doing some business for my dad," said the man. "This and that."

"That's pretty cool," said Sage. "I like to see families stick together after the kids grow up. He a good man to work for?"

"The best," said the stranger. "What're *you* doing out here?"

For some reason Sage was feeling confidential. Though he didn't usually tell people much about what he was doing, he felt comfortable with this stranger and decided to share some of his story.

"Well, I'm a writer, and I do okay, but I got sick of the city and all the bull. And it bothers me, you know, the things I read in the papers. You know, people hurting puppies and blowing each other up and all that. I just kind of can't stand it. Really."

Sage was surprised at himself. He was not usually this inarticulate. "So, I decided to come out here where a man can think and try to do something about it all. I suppose that sounds silly to you."

"No, not really," said the man. "You just keep knocking and that door'll open, you'll see. Keep looking—you'll find what you're looking for."

"*That sounds familiar too*, thought Sage. *"Knock and it shall be . . ."* No, he couldn't quite get it. Something from long, long ago. Good advice, anyway. Perhaps meeting this guy would be a good omen for his quest.

"Thanks," said Sage, "Thanks, I will. Have a good trip, now," he added, seeing that the stranger was getting up to leave.

"Same to you," the man said, smiling as he went out the door.

That was a nice fellow, thought Sage. *Kind of a shine about him. Maybe I'll see him again sometime.*

CHAPTER
FOUR

**LEXANDER PREISCZECH WAS** confused when he came to the United States from Eastern Europe, and the longer he stayed, the more confused he got. One of the most confusing things was the supermarket.

He'd try to buy something simple, like soap, and find himself confronted with a 40-foot-long aisle containing nothing *but* soap. There was Fresh Off An Irish Clothesline Soap and Manly Man Soap and Pamper Yourself, You Deserve It Soap. There was Original Regular with a Hint of Mint and New Improved All-Day Protection and Gold Star Special with holographic packaging. He hadn't seen Extra Crispy yet, but it wouldn't have surprised him. All he wanted was a damned bar of soap, just soap in a white package with black writing that said SOAP, or maybe in a barrel and you'd pull a hunk of it out for yourself. These pointless choices, embracing every product, confused him to the point of paralysis.

It was also hard to concentrate in the supermarket when people kept playing games and making fun of him—because he was a foreigner, obviously. And he didn't understand how they knew his name, but they always did. He'd tried switching supermarkets, but sooner or later it always started up again.

"Preisczech! Preisczech!" someone would call, usually over a loudspeaker. Palms sweating, fighting for control, he would present himself at the counter.

"Yes?"

"What?"

Their incomprehension was mutual. "You called me."

"I did no such thing!"

"But I'm Preisczech!"

"Oh, ha ha, you're a great comedian, now go away."

What kind of game was that to play on a man, to call him and call him and then pretend you've never spoken his name? And in every store, every single store, if he went there long enough, some stranger knew his name and blasted it out for everyone to hear.

It was the government, he knew. They had found out somehow and they were trying to break him down.

AFTER SIX MONTHS of this torment, Preisczech took the radical step of changing his name. He did not change it legally, of course, since this would have drawn even more attention and confirmed official suspicions. But he changed the name he *told* people. He procured false identification—not a difficult feat for someone trained in the deceits and shadow economies of his native land.

"Danger is my middle name," said the well-known American axiom. Well, maybe it could be a first name as well. Not literally, of course, but it got him thinking. He did want something daring and intrepid sounding, but not too strange. Something pointed, like an arrow, sharp and piercing. He wanted to carve out the instrument of his new destiny—his name—carefully and with concentration, like an indigenous person readying himself for the hunt. This cluster of ideas taken together suggested a particularly suitable name—distinctive, but also easy to pronounce.

As a last name, he wanted something solid sounding, dependable and trustworthy, simple and a little aristocratic. A multicultural man with ancestors from many nations, Preisczech had had a German-Jewish grandmother named "Stein." Rendered in American as "Stone," it was eminently suitable.

Full of pleased anticipation, Preisczech left his rented room with its competing smells of cabbage, tortillas, and curry. His destination was the biker bar two blocks from his place of residence.

It has been said that bikers are not what they once were, not what their reputation suggests, or once suggested. Bikers are respectable business persons, solid citizens, normal middle-to-upper-class gentlemen and ladies who pursue this interesting hobby on weekends—people who wash frequently and have no criminal records.

The denizens of the Dirty Dog were not that kind of biker. Preisczech had developed a friendship with them based on their amusement at his utter cluelessness. To wit, he was not afraid of them. They loved him for his entertainment value. His dumb-foreigner-type questions provided a welcome change from the usual drinking, fighting, and drug taking—an intellectual form of enjoyment.

Preisczech was excited as he prepared to re-encounter these friends. He had never told them his name, so the opportunity was perfect. They were a tough audience, and this was, in a small way, his opening night. If the name passed muster with *them*, there was nothing to fear.

With studied casualness, Preisczech stepped from bright sunlight into a netherworld of small neon signs, dreamlike characters, and a fog of smoke and stale beer. There were windows, but you wouldn't have known it; they hadn't been cleaned in decades. Standing around the pool table, sitting on barstools or lying across them, hassling the bartender and each other, oiled hair and leather jackets gleaming gently in the half-light, the denizens of this limbo waited, unaware that they were about to participate in the rebirth of Preisczech.

Advancing a few careful steps into the room, he stood in expectation, a locus of electric silence that drew their eyes, impervious though they were. Because Preisczech had seen a number of James Bond films, he now assumed a dramatic 007 stance.

"The name's Stone," he said, pausing a moment for emphasis. "Flint Stone."

The raucous laughter was a hurricane, a typhoon, a nor'easter from the Arctic that carried Preisczech, stumbling and crimson-faced, all the way back to the smell of cabbage and sambusas. The scent of his temporary home wafted over him, covering his shame. What in God's name had he done wrong now? How could he ever understand these ridiculous people and their impossible and contradictory language? He had briefly attended an ESL class, a humorous thing in itself because, speaking five languages as he did, English was hardly his "second language." He momentarily considered *thought, through, though, throw,* and *threw,* and shuddered.

Back at the Dirty Dog, the laughter continued for fully five minutes. The bikers treasured Preisczech. They were sure he was insane. They began joking about all the silly things he had done, like that cigar box he carried everywhere. One time, early in their acquaintance, the gang had stolen it. Ruby had distracted Preisczech, who had an eye for a pretty face, by cleaning her three-inch-long red fingernails with a six-inch-bladed knife.

(How she managed to steer a motorcycle with those things was a mystery.) With a howl of triumph, Wolf had grabbed the box from under Preisczech's arm and danced away with it.

Preisczech guarded that box so closely, the gang was sure it contained money or jewels. He was not the type to have a box full of drugs, which would have been the third possibility. When they failed to open it with knives, chains, heavy boots, and even a pickaxe (kindly provided by Bill the bartender), they resorted to playing keep-away with it.

It did not really strike them as strange that the box was impenetrable, though the cheap-looking wood should have shattered under one good stomp from a heavy boot. They were not the sort to wonder about such things, their emotions being limited to anger, amusement, satisfaction, comradeship, and occasional self-pity. They saw this as just one more proof that the man was insane. Why have a stupid box you can't open? Ruby alone was intrigued. She raised one winged eyebrow a quarter of an inch and contemplated Preisczech. There was something here worth investigating.

PREISCZECH WAS *NOT* insane, and not an idiot either, though this was the second most popular verdict. Nor was he even what used to be called an "idiot savant" as some people back home had thought, though this was nearer to the truth. Preisczech was just a little different. In a foreign country, trying too hard to be cool, and a little different. The denizens of the Dirty Dog did not know that the object of their laughter, though still under thirty, had degrees in engineering and nuclear physics from the cream of European universities. Nor would they have cared. He was still an idiot.

A week after the embarrassment about his new name, Preisczech tried again, remembering something about getting back on a horse after you fall off (though in his industrialized region he had rarely seen a horse and never ridden one).

He had decided to introduce himself with a last name only. This would sound tough and competent; a first name could come later. In the construction of this name, he used a time-honored method, dissecting and recombining bits of his *current* names. He took one syllable from his first name, Alexander, and another from his middle name, Lazlo. This time there would be no silly slip-ups, no unwitting allusions to cartoon characters. His new name was snappy and distinctive and pleased him greatly. It had a dashing quality, slightly exotic with the requisite hint of danger.

Yet again he stepped into the bar and walked forward, while the bikers waited with bated breath (in some cases literally, since a bet that morning had facilitated the consumption of the entire contents of a terrified fisherman's bait box.)

"The name's Lazlex," Preisczech intoned.

"Ex-Lax!" roared Buzzard, Snake Eyes, Wolf, Beaner, Ruby, and Skull. "The name's Ex-Lax!" they cried in sheer joy, bowing and shaking hands with each other and doffing imaginary top hats, introducing themselves and their friends.

It doesn't matter, Preisczech told himself desperately. *It doesn't matter.* Coolness was the least of his problems. He was here to get a job done.

ACROSS THE STREET in their nondescript, dark van, Drake and Muldoon suddenly sat up. In an instant, it was all worthwhile: the bad food and worse, the loneliness, the endless stakeouts, the crushing boredom. Two years they had waited, and now, at last, it was paying off.

Muldoon punched up headquarters on his cell phone. "You were right, sir," he said. "One of them has broken cover at last. Yes—Project Lazlex."

CHAPTER
FIVE

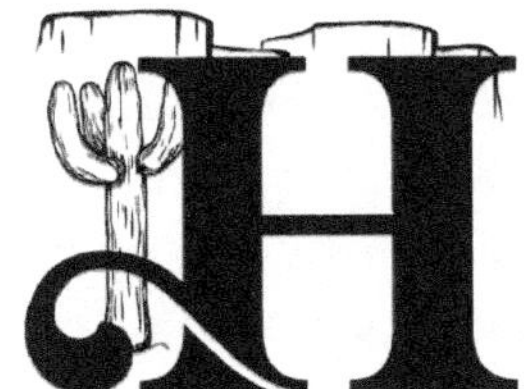**ALYCON SAGE SAT** in his motel room watching television. No-Name Stupid was watching too, a look of disgust on his aristocratic face. The Arabs and the Israelis were kicking the snot out of each other as usual, and Iran and America had horned in, making everything worse. Halycon Sage had tried to understand the Middle East situation and failed. He had read several books on it and had friends on both sides of the seemingly unbridgeable divide between the Israeli position and the Palestinian one but saw no solution.

He tended to agree with whoever was talking, though their viewpoints were mutually exclusive. He would have liked to get a couple of them together so he could hear both sides at once, but it seemed like a bad idea, since they hated each other's guts. The moderates and peace activists—Muslims, Christians, Jews, and others—might have done something, but with all the bombings and shootings and arrests and demolitions and rocket attacks from both sides, their stock was lower than camel scat.

He flipped the channel. Shopping. By means of an amazing breakthrough for mankind, it was now possible to buy a diamond cell phone for ninety thousand dollars. He flipped again. A hospital in East Africa. Thin, dark, patient men were lying on a concrete floor. These sick men not only had no beds of any kind, they didn't even have a blanket. Perhaps if they had a diamond cell phone, they could sell it and buy some blankets.

He flipped again, then turned toward his horse. "Iraq?" he asked No-Name Stupid. Stupid gave him a look that said, *Don't even get me started.*

After a few days of riding through sagebrush and Joshua trees, over alpine meadows and up and down small mountains, Halycon Sage was watching television again. He found it relaxing. Besides, it was a break from considering how a man with a brown and white pinto, a reasonable income, a modest literary gift and an international reputation could save the world. Also, though he may have been imagining it, it seemed to him that No-Name Stupid sulked when Sage did not join him in his nightly pursuit. There was a reproachful quality about the way the horse chewed his oatmeal cookie.

Avoiding the news, they settled on an old western.

"White Man speak with forked tongue," declared the scowling villain.

"You tell 'em, brother!" cried Sage, who had had a few beers. "You clowns listen to that guy! Drive 'em into the sea! Don't let 'em get a toe hold!"

"White Man *brother*," said the wise and benevolent old peace chief, a man who obviously deserved the trust of the tribe far more than the grumpy, unfriendly bad guy. "Big Chief in Washington say White Man bring peace, prosperity, school choice, and no new taxes."

Sage blinked. He had apparently dozed off and imagined that last part. He thought of a quote he had once read from Sherman Alexie, "The only thing more pathetic than Indians on TV is Indians *watching* Indians on TV." So why was he even watching this stuff? What did Stupid see in it?

"The Big Chief in Washington wants to live in peace with his Indian brothers," said the guileful White Man in the nice, clean Stetson. "If you sign a treaty with us, your land will be protected as long as the sun rises and the moon sets, as long as the otter swims and the wind blows the prairie grass and the buffalo roams the plains!"

"Not bloody long, then," remarked Sage, opening another beer.

"No! Me make WAR!" exclaimed the stubborn villain, bad sport that he was.

The Indians always sound so stupid in these old shows, thought Sage. But of course that's the way anyone sounds speaking an unfamiliar language. "'Scuse please, you know what time is? Me Bill! Me of *America*!" Just once Sage would like to see the translation go the other way, with the Whites speaking an Indian language.

"You not fight, we make good for you," says the White ambassador. "I'm dreadfully sorry, old fellow," says the chief, "I certainly take your point, but a strong minority opinion within our community holds that you would fail to keep your word."

"As long as the bats fly," the man from Washington was babbling. "As long as the woodchuck runs, and the ground hog pops out of his hole ..."

Halycon Sage raised his beer in a toast. "As long as the billboards loom from horizon to horizon," he mumbled. "As long as the plastic bags rattle in the wind, as long as the neon glitters and shines. As long as the juke box plays and the workers are exploited, the land will be ruled by the rich, so that government of the money, by the money, and for the money shall not perish from the earth."

And No-Name Stupid, who usually maintained the stoic silence befitting a traditional Indian pony, let out a loud neigh, followed by something that certainly sounded like a burp.

Got to keep him out of that beer, thought Halycon Sage. As for himself, he really, really had to break this television habit, Stupid or no Stupid. The horse could just pout; it would be good for him to find some productive activity instead. The problem was, Stupid couldn't exactly go for a gallop around the block, now could he? He was more or less confined to the motel rooms, and there wasn't a lot for a horse to do in there. A horse couldn't knit, for instance.

But focusing on himself once again, a favorite topic when he wasn't considering the state of the world and possible solutions, Sage knew that the television was worse for him than the alcohol, worse than the junk food. It was soothing on a superficial level, but it sapped his strength and robbed his dreams of meaning. His mind was becoming a scratchy recording device that played back mediocre hit songs he didn't even like, news of bombings and shootings, the faces of annoying celebrities. *As a man thinketh, so is he.* And he had better start thinketh-ing something constructive or he was done for. The problem was, he had already had every conceivable thought at least five or six times, and they all conflicted with each other.

And incidentally, he thought for about the fiftieth time, *when did people decide by some magic consensus that it was okay to refer to them as "consumers"? Did I miss the vote on that one?*

Not human beings or living beings. Not men, women, and children. Not souls, or spirits created from the breath of God, or free individuals with existential choice. Not even citizens. Consumers.

It sounded to Halycon Sage like nothing so much as feedlot cows being stuffed up for the slaughter. They were supposed to buy, buy, buy instead of eat, eat, eat. Their awesome, God-given freedom of choice was reduced to the choice between Brand X and Brand Y, and when they were killed and gutted at the end, money was supposed to pour out. Or, even better, they were bled daily like Masai cattle so that the money would dribble out slowly, generating interest.

Halycon Sage wondered how many of the people who thought and felt as he did had died insane. *Bummer*, thought Halycon Sage.

CHAPTER
SIX

**FTER HIS SECOND** setback, Preisczech could not face home, with its cabbage and curry smells and its muffled silence. Not the dirty wallpaper nor the kindly landlady—none of it. Some perverse instinct made him return to the *other* scene of his humiliations, the supermarket. And that is how he was picked up by Halycon Sage, who had come in to purchase a box of Instant Quaker Oats for No-Name Stupid, who would not eat real oats but only instant ones, along with the occasional Pop Tart. Feeding him cost a fortune.

Sage found Preisczech staring like a frozen fish and unable to utter a single word. The kindly Sage, who was occasionally mad himself and frequently depressed, took

Preisczech by the elbow like a good nurse and shepherded him out into the cool, sweet night. No-Name Stupid waited, finicky in the matter of food, but indifferent as to the addition of a second rider.

Later, after stomachs were full and the campfire in the vacant lot had subsided to a gentle crackling, Preisczech spoke.

"I've invented something."

"I have too," said Halycon Sage happily. "I invent things every day. Last weekend I invented *Boo Radley Goes Hawaiian*. Fine summer reading. Watch for the movie."

"No," said Preisczech, "Not like that. I've really invented something."

"What is it?" asked Halycon Sage.

Suddenly, in a phenomenon familiar to all who speak foreign languages badly, the tired Preisczech's English deserted him completely.

"When think go boom, it doesn't," he said.

"Come again?" asked Sage.

"Think go boom," said Preisczech loudly, hoping volume could compensate for lack of vocabulary. "Car engine. Plane engine. Firecracker. Gun. No go. Just sit there."

"Do you mean," asked Sage, slowly turning to face his strange new friend, "that your invention stops explosions?"

"Explosions!" cried Preisczech happily. "Yes! One hundred meters, two hundred meters from my machine, no explosions. Nothing. Just sit there."

"Bombs?" asked Sage. "IED's?"

"No bombs," said Preisczech solemnly. "Big, little, make no difference. Sit there like cement. Terrorist bombs, insurgent bombs, brave guerilla fighter bombs, fighting for freedom bombs, smart bombs, stupid bombs, blow-peasant's-leg-off-in-a-good-cause bombs, Serb bombs, Bosnian Bombs, make no difference. Sit there."

"Nuclear bombs?"

"Two hundred megaton bombs, hydrogen bombs, bunker busters and daisy cutters," said Preisczech lyrically, his English returning in the enthusiasm of sharing his great secret.

"Jeez," said Halycon Sage slowly. "Dude, we've got to talk."

A TERRIBLE THING had happened to Basel Vasselschnauzer: his editor had told him to get up off his ass and go out and do some research. No one had ever talked to Basel Vasselschnauzer in this way, fearing the scattershot malice of his tongue and pen. But now he had brought it on himself by making up one too many interviews, this time with a lion-maned author of undoubted integrity who hotly denied ever speaking with him.

People did not confront Vasselschnauzer for his irresponsible behavior because they feared him. He was a loose cannon that might strike anywhere on the slightest provocation, and he circulated his barbed comments widely in the bars and cafes that mattered, where they were picked up by gleeful gossip columnists. But for once the editor was too angry to care.

For the first time in years, Vasselschnauzer had to leave the luxurious apartment where he wrote his column, that cocoon of safety, that idyllic place of green silk cushions, black marble pillars and well-stocked bar. While he did not need money, he *did* need the column, which enabled him to keep up the pretense that he was doing something. And, as if all this weren't bad enough, he was supposed to go and find Halycon Sage. Sure. Catch the wind in a butterfly net. Bring home some starlight in a little glass jar. Go find Halycon Sage.

D RAKE AND MULDOON had discovered Project Lazlex while trolling the internet, two of many bored agents stuck in front of computers in some nameless office belonging to a nameless agency. Well, it was supposed to be nameless, but it was the NSA, of course, or Homeland Security, or whatever it was by now. If the agency could be imagined, for one moment, as hell, then Drake and Muldoon occupied the furthest reaches of its outer darkness. The week they discovered Project Lazlex, five of their colleagues were fired for watching pornography, playing online video games, surreptitiously working on home businesses, or obsessively emailing an aunt in Wichita.

One might think the motionless hours in the black van would have provided some relief from the motionless hours in the windowless basement—a change of scene, at least. But this was not the case. Supposedly suspicious foreigners who never actually did anything were no more interesting than the stupefying deluge of web content.

Most of the online trolling was done by sophisticated computer programs that sifted millions of websites and emails for words of likely interest to terrorists. But a tiny percentage needed the further attention of a human eye, albeit a bored and underpaid one. Some of the stuff was amusing. Drake and Muldoon had viewed "Osama Yo Mama," and, for some incomprehensible reason, "The Lama Song," which apparently resembled some kind of code with its cryptic statements and frantic repetitions of, "Lama, lama, *duck*!" Was that maybe a reference to those "duck and cover" drills from the 1950s? Were they really talking about nuclear bombs?

Most of the material was deadly dull: wannabe revolutionaries, survivalists who probably couldn't survive a night in the backyard, hate-filled racists and isolationists with bad punctuation, and endless diatribes about the proper length of beards and trousers from the Wahabi-leaning Muslim websites.

What if a man couldn't *grow* a beard? And could the trousers just *touch* the ankle, or did they have to be completely clear of it? A saying of Muhammad was cited, admonishing those who "wore their trousers low in pride." One valiant participant vainly pointed out that the admonition was about pride, not about pants. But the nitpicking discussion went on, oblivious. And Muldoon thought if he read one more word about The Veil, he would tear off his *own* clothes and run screaming into the street, giving them something else for their discussions of modesty.

Drake had just scarfed down his last doughnut and was counting the minutes till break, when he could go and get a candy bar. Suddenly the words "Project Lazlex" popped up, brilliant yellow in the middle of a black screen. "Look at this," he said, elbowing his neighbor.

Muldoon looked. Drake clicked on the entrance portal and read more glowing letters. "TOP SECRET," it said. "Enter at your own risk! Triple-Protected. Password, please." Drake began mechanically entering numbers designed to break the barrier. "In," he said. For the pathetic amount of training he'd had, Drake was not too bad.

"This looks like it was designed by a 13-year-old," he muttered.

"That's not a nice way to talk about your colleagues," said Muldoon, convinced they had found yet another secret U.S. government site. "They make a lot more money than you do."

"Project Lazlex," read the next screen. "From the many come the few! The few who will win! The many who will take over the world, and the few who will rule through them!"

"What's this drivel?" asked Drake, removing the World's Largest Piece of Dandruff from his indeterminately brown hair. "See, I told you it was kids."

"No way," stated Muldoon, feeling a rising excitement in his throat. "Look at this." Now a map of the world had appeared in blue, green, and brown, complete with latitude and longitude lines. Colorfully red and silver, hundreds of tiny robots scurried everywhere. But it was not any of this that made Muldoon sit up. The symbols toward which the tiny robots were hurrying appeared to represent real underground missile sites.

IT WAS SHEER bad luck that Josh and Trevor had picked the name "Lazlex" for the computer game they were designing, a game in which tiny robots attacked nuclear missiles.

"Hacker *extraordinaire!*" Trevor had gloated. He was really *very* good. He had discovered the actual locations of the sites, some of which were supposed to be top secret. He figured this verisimilitude would increase interest when the game went live. A simple version had been up for months, building awareness, but it was almost time to unveil the real thing.

"I am a genius. You may touch my feet."

"I *may* touch your stinky feet," replied Josh, "right after hell freezes over. You may wash my *socks.*"

"Get your *sister* to wash your socks," said Trevor, knowing Josh's weak spot. Josh's sister was better at everything than he was except within his narrow but brilliant purview of scientific and computer geekery.

"I've kept our identities secret for months," bragged Trevor. "People are going crazy looking for us, but they can't trace it back. I bet even the *NSA* couldn't find us."

"Dude, they could *find* you, they just don't *want* you."

"They want your socks for a secret weapon," said Trevor.

Josh changed the subject. "Let's get back to work. We have to get this thing done by Friday."

"Lazlex" was a compromise. Josh was a Superman aficionado with a particular *tendresse* for Lex Luthor. Trevor had recently been designing a new laser gun. Both of them thought "Project Lazlex" sounded cool.

It was bad luck that the game involved tiny robots, and further bad luck that it also involved nuclear weapons silos. And it was the most final and devastating piece of bad luck that the budgeting department overseeing the nameless bunker had decided to spend a sudden windfall, not on something sensible like chairs that wouldn't drive the agents mad with squeaking every time they moved, but on a single special instrument that not only saw through walls, but did it microscopically.

If none of these things had happened, Alexander Preisczech would never have come to the attention of various governments in the way that he did, Halycon Sage could have continued wandering the hills and deserts of the west eating Twinkies, and Basel Vasselschnauzer could have gone to sleep between his green silk sheets instead of becoming the most annoying kidnap victim in the history of the universe.

"WON'T WORK," SAID Sage to Preisczech matter-of-factly.

"What do you mean, won't work?"

"Your invention."

"Is tested," said Preisczech testily.

"I mean, maybe the mechanics work, but there are some problems you haven't considered."

"Like what?" inquired Preisczech. His English was becoming more colloquial and free-flowing through his constant campfire and motel room discussions with his new found friend.

"Well, if bombs can't explode, other kinds of explosions can't happen either. Like the internal combustion engine. Cars won't run. Airplanes won't fly."

"Me, I have considered this already," said Preisczech relaxing. He'd been worried that Sage really had something. "Cars no work, airplanes no work—too bad. Can't fly out to see grandma during long weekend, very sad. But also, no planes fly over dropping bombs, no 1.24 million traffic deaths a year. Just once in a while, somebody gets run over by wagon."

"Have you ever *seen* anyone who's been run over by a wagon?" asked Sage, who had.

"That is not the point," said Preisczech, hurriedly steering the subject from the concrete back toward the abstract. Neither of them could stand the sight of blood—perhaps this was one more reason they were friends. They could hardly take out a splinter. It was not exactly cowardice; it was an overdose of empathy.

"There are always trade-offs," said Preisczech, who had learned this word on the internet. It struck him as an elegant concept. "Win some, lose some. Give a little, get a little. Take—"

"Okay, I get the point," said Sage hurriedly, trying to forestall any more tinpot philosophy. "But what about electricity? None of the coal-fired plants would work, would they? Natural gas-powered stuff wouldn't work. You couldn't even strike a match!"

"Don't need match," muttered Preisczech sullenly, but he knew he was whipped. This was the idiot savant aspect of his genius; he could get so involved in a line of research that he didn't see the most obvious things that were outside the laser beam of his immediate focus, things a middle school science student would have thought of. In this he was the exact opposite of Sage, whose vision was so broad and all-encompassing that he could never bear to draw boundaries anywhere and his best ideas dribbled off into puddles of infinitude. Perhaps this was how they would save the world, by compensating for each other, two flawed geniuses supplementing each other's deficiencies.

Preisczech wandered away from the campfire, mumbling and scratching. When he did not return for three days, Halycon Sage began to worry about something. Not that he had been lost or injured. No. That he might be inventing something even worse.

THE SAYING, "THERE is nothing to fear but fear itself," had puzzled Preisczech since his university days. It had a Catch–22[1] quality about it. Apparently, it was supposed to be reassuring, but if you *had no* fear, it was unnecessary, and therefore useless. You just went ahead being brave and/or stupid, doing daring things while tossing off a hearty laugh. If, on the other hand, you were truly terrified, you had lots and lots of the one thing that, according to the saying, was actually worth being afraid of. In other words, any time you were really and terribly afraid, your fears were justified.

The saying merely served to magnify the fear. *Thank you very much for nothing, Mr. Franklin Delano Roosevelt,* thought Preisczech. The whole issue, then, was whether or not it was possible to overcome fear by will power, and the jury was still out on that one.

It has also been said that one who does not know fear is incapable of being brave, because courage is the overcoming of fear. Preisczech had though a lot about all this, because he had a lot of anxiety. Lately he was terrified of two things: losing the cigar box, and losing the dented tin whistle he had taken to wearing around his neck.

The whistle was a new addition, as was the current content of the cigar box. If he lost the cigar box, all his plans would come to nothing. But if he lost the whistle, cheap though it looked, humanity had better go and find itself a new planet, because life on this one would not be worth living.

---

1. A "catch-22" is a common phrase for a certain type of impossible situation, taken from Joseph Heller's novel Catch-22. In the book, anyone who didn't want to go home from the war was crazy and could go home, but if he decided to avail himself of this opportunity, he was no longer crazy, because now he wanted to go home, so he couldn't go.

CHAPTER
SEVEN

UBY WAS HAVING a really bad day. She slammed her whiskey glass down irritably. It was still half full, a thing not known to have happened before. (Optimists say the glass is half full, pessimists say it's half empty, but Ruby generally said, "It's half empty, so fill it up.")

She turned her honed scowl on Wolf, raised the amazing eyebrow its customary quarter inch and said, "Why don't you grow up?"

Wolf paused, glass in midair, in contemplation of this stunningly new concept. He wasn't sure what she meant.

"And by that you mean . . ." he inquired, emphasizing his puzzlement with a graceful wave of one hand, which was slightly spoiled by the large "Mudda" tattooed on his shoulder.

Grow up! Stop hanging around in the dark getting stoned! Go out and get a freakin' job!" shouted Ruby angrily.

"The word "job" had not been mentioned in the Dirty Dog before, at least not in conjunction with any serious suggestion of honest paid work. The boys sat a moment in stunned silence, then decided Ruby was joking. They thought the joke was not too bad for one-thirty in the afternoon and broke into roars of laughter, laughter that Alexander Preisczech would have recognized only too well.

"Oh, the hell with all of you!" cried Ruby, suddenly and inexplicably reaching some sort of apotheosis of life-style change. "I'm outta here!" And she was. Out the door with a bang, into the unaccustomed sunlight.

This was unheard of. The Dirty Dog gang had been together for many years. They had changed from this house to that apartment to the other houseboat, garage, park or even city or state, but they always moved in a body and nobody ever left, or even threatened to leave. They were so used to each other that they moved as one organic being. Generally they ventured out of the bars only at night. Sometimes they bought supplies or did unavoidable errands, and sometimes they indulged in antiquated rumbles with the only other gang willing to pretend that guns did not exist—that pipes, chains, and switchblades were still state of the art. The Dirty Dogs and the Fifth Street Mofos were avoided by the younger and more up-to-date gangs, who thought they were crazy old coots living in a time warp. This was true.

Though the two gangs had been sworn enemies for as long as they could remember (not long in some cases, due to the amounts of various substances they ingested), they generally did not hurt each other too seriously. They defended their pathetically small pieces of turf, passing them back and forth, and indulged in witty practical jokes at each other's expense. When they died, probably of old age, they would all attend each other's funerals.

Thus Ruby, by her manner of exiting but even more by her serious mention of the words "grow up" and "job," was violating decades of tradition. It just wasn't done. Nice people did not act like that.

"Fools! Idiots!" fumed Ruby.

Ruby was an odd bird. The years of hard living had destroyed neither her beauty nor her intelligence. Perhaps this was because her dissolute life was largely pretense. The Dirty Dogs, each involved in his own drama, had not really noticed that Ruby rarely used drugs and did not sleep around. Nor had they noticed that her glass was generally full of ginger ale, that her reputation as a two-fisted drinker was largely based on the frequent slamming of soda pop. Only Bill the bartender was in on the secret.

Many a time, Ruby had slipped out of the Dirty Dog to read and think, to run, to practice *tai chi* and *chi gong*. It was only her *dramatic* exit that was noticed. Her brief and frequent absences fell beneath the radar screens of her dimwitted companions. God knows why she'd lived with them all this time—a sense of safety perhaps. But she also had this other, secret life.

What Ruby really loved was motorcycles. She was an expert rider, even a trick rider, who had been known to enter contests and win. The other thing she loved was reading, and when her turn came to do the unavoidable errands, she invariably went to the library. But staying away too long from the Dirty Dog and the Dirty Dog Boys would have given her away. (The guys hung out in the bar all day and fought and partied all night. No one but the gang themselves knew when they slept, or even exactly where they lived.) Because her love of reading fiction could have conflicted with her need to maintain her image, she particularly enjoyed short novels. *Very* short novels. Her favorite author, it will come as no surprise, was Halycon Sage.

No-NAME STUPID was on the lam. He loved Halycon Sage, but he loved his freedom more. Going out of his mind with boredom in another cheap motel, he had seen his chance and bolted out the door, not even pausing to neigh goodbye. Down the grassy side road he galloped, enjoying the smells of early morning. The dew sparkled on the spring-green grass and he stopped to nibble some. It was the healthiest thing he'd eaten in weeks ...

No, rewind—he didn't either. Not even succumbing to the sweet succulent odor of the year's tenderest grass, he galloped on. The grass-nibbling had been a brief fantasy cascading through his mind, almost real in its clarity, but evanescent. Stupid was on a mission, and it wasn't Halycon Sage's mission either. He didn't care about saving the world or understanding it or finding himself or babysitting Preisczech or any of that stuff. He just wanted to be free and out of doors and perhaps, after a suitable time had passed, to find a nice female horse.

Stupid galloped from the side road onto a larger road. Drivers stared in surprise as they whizzed by in their cars, trucks, and SUVs. Stupid galloped from the larger road to a main thoroughfare. And reaching speeds that were new to him, intoxicated by the freedom and the running, not unaware of human things, but uncaring, No-Name Stupid galloped straight onto the freeway.

Though he was not from New Hampshire, Stupid held to their motto, "Live free or die!" He did not think in words, but these were his sentiments. *Live free or die!* thought No-Name Stupid, not in words. *Live free or die!*

A HORSE ON the *freeway*, thought Ruby. *That's unusual.* She was a quick thinker, so quick that there was time, before she acted, for a flash of memory. She'd been fifteen the first time she sat on a motorcycle. It was a Harley, the property of a neighbor. The young neighbor had been showing off—because even then, Ruby had been beautiful. That she leaped onto the slowly moving motorcycle was no surprise. Any young girl of a certain type would be attracted by the roaring machine and the black leather, the superior smile and the promise of speed and freedom. Jumping onto and riding away on a slowly moving motorcycle was no big deal for a quick-thinking girl whose coordination had always been extraordinary. What was unusual was that she did it standing up.

The memory flashed before her and away. It was the twenty-first century and there was still a horse on the freeway. Fortunately, there was plenty of shoulder on the road and the horse was, so far, sticking to it.

Ruby loved her Harley; she hated even to scratch it, but this was an emergency. In an instant, Ruby calculated time and distance, the speed of the horse and the effect of the wind, angles and trajectories. Then, ditching her motorcycle as gently as possible (not very), she leaped onto the back of No-Name Stupid.

Stupid galloped on, surprised but interested. This new rider was light and standing up, a trick Halycon Sage had never mastered, despite his Indian blood and his hours of secret practice. She had that telepathy a few people have with horses, horse and rider as one. She slid to a sitting position as his gallop slowed to a canter. *Let's go, horse*, she thought. *We'll head for the exit. The freeway is no place for us.*

Alright, thought Stupid. *It's too loud here anyway. I was scared.* These thoughts were transmitted through the subtle moves of horse and rider. Ruby held the thick, glistening mane, gently steering. She knew what she was doing, not like Halycon Sage, who rode around in circles eating Cheetos and looking for Truth. Her calm strength communicated itself to the willing horse. *Safe at last.*

There's an old saying, "The horse knows the way." Maybe it was even the title of a play. Anyway, No-Name Stupid *did* know the way. Much to his own surprise, as his gallop slowed so did his sense of adventure and rebellion. It was all very well to go galloping off into who knows where, but it was nice to come back again.

Under Ruby's firm but gentle guidance, which did nothing more than steer him away from the busiest streets, Stupid found himself heading for the tree-lined road leading to the latest edge-of-town motel. He stopped now and then to munch the sweet green grass he'd dreamed about before. It was better than doughnuts, better than oatmeal cookies. *We're going about this wrong*, thought Stupid. *Too much TV, too much junk food, too much beer. We need to be riding out where the air is free, not sitting around in the air conditioning.* He clopped along contentedly, in no hurry, but bound for home. He'd have to talk to Halycon Sage about cleaning up their act.

RUBY WAS SURPRISED when No–Name Stupid turned into the scruffy parking lot of the Desert Inn Motel. The poplar trees swayed in the wind, leaves flashing like silver coins as their shiny upper and dull lower sides were alternately exposed to the sun. The wind was light and fresh and the willow trees waved and sighed. High desert clouds moved majestically across the wide blue sky, taking their time. It was a beautiful day. On a day like this, with the whole world to explore, why would a horse go to a motel room? For the horse obviously had a particular room in mind. He stopped most firmly in front of the door to Room 10. The door was battered wood, and the zero of the ten was falling off and sat askew. *Interesting*, thought Ruby, and knocked.

When the door opened, she saw an Indian man with a tired face. He looked kind. He was just a little handsome, and there was humor in his face. He looked noble somehow, and tired, and a bit beaten down, as if he had seen everything and didn't know what to do about it. "Hello Stupid," said the man.

An odd greeting, thought Ruby, then saw that he was talking to the horse. At the same moment, the man appeared to realize that he might have seemed insulting. "That's my horse," he explained. "No-Name Stupid."

"Oh," said Ruby, noncommittal.

The man looked her up and down, not the way a man looks at a woman, but the way a philosopher looks at a new phenomenon, or a traveler at a mountain, detached but curious. The horse walked casually into the motel room, as if he did this every day.

"Come on in," said Halycon Sage. And she did.

CHAPTER
EIGHT

"**S**o, you're looking for God or something?" Ruby asked the man in the motel room. Though she had never seen him before, she felt immediately at ease. They were settled comfortably on the couch with glasses of ginger ale. Ruby was pleased that this strange man had her favorite drink on hand.

"Not God exactly," said Sage. "I already found God, but I lost Him again. He's around here somewhere, though. He never goes away. It's like when you close your eyes and you can't see the room anymore. It's still there."

"Huh," said Ruby, a woman of few words. She thought about it. "So you're looking for Truth, trying to find yourself, trying to find the meaning of life?"

"I know all that stuff too," said Sage. "Been there, done that. I'm trying to save the world."

"And just how are you doing that?" asked Ruby.

Riding around in circles eating Cheetos, thought Stupid.

"Well, I came out here where a man can think clearly, where the air is clean and there's no Basel Vasselschnauzer."

"Gesundheit," said Ruby automatically, wondering if he had a sinus condition.

"No, no that's a guy. Trust me, you don't want to meet him. Anyway, I came out here to be where things are real, so I could plan my next step, you know?"

Ruby nodded.

"But I don't seem to be getting anywhere. Stupid and I have gotten off the track, somehow. We don't know what we're doing."

You don't, thought Stupid. *Speak for yourself.*

"Why don't you do some spiritual practices?" asked Ruby. "Chi Gong. Yoga. Meditation. Get your head straight."

"I did all that twenty years ago," said Sage. "It would be going backward."

Ruby thought about it.

"Okay, well, you're an Indian, aren't you?"

"Sort of," said Sage.

"So you're supposed to know some stuff, aren't you?"

Supposed to, thought No-Name Stupid, who was enjoying the conversation.

Sage was silent. He thought back to one of his heroes, Larry Cloud Morgan. Now there was an Indian who really did "know some stuff." He was an Ojibwa Pipe Carrier who had dedicated his life to peace work and had received five years in prison for symbolically attacking a nuclear weapons silo with a hammer. Many were grateful to him for making the obvious point that these things should be dismantled. That he made his point in an active way, not merely with words, was an expression of his Indian culture, just as, in the early 1980's, another group of Indians had sailed a small boat to Spain, planted a flag and claimed it for their own.

Halycon Sage had attended Larry's funeral. He had not known him well, but had given him a ride once as they talked pleasantly and had walked behind him another time in a ceremony—directly behind him, walking in his footsteps. This ceremony had been part of something called the Harmonic Convergence, an event based on Mayan prophecies. Evidently the harmonies had not converged yet, at least from what Sage could see. The world was supposed to be saved pretty soon according to several dovetailing predictions, but the whole thing looked like an unmitigated disaster to him. That was why he had decided to be like Larry Cloud Morgan and try doing a bit of it himself.

At Larry's funeral, the body was beautifully dressed in full tribal regalia, laid out in leatherwork, beading, turquoise and all kinds of adornments, with his sacred pipe in his hands. The corpse looked about twice as alive as any of the people in the room—not because they were less alive, but because he seemed so much more so. Sage had never seen anything like it. The "prepared" dead people he'd come across before looked like slightly decadent wax dolls getting ready for a hot date, but this body was like a charged battery, conveying not only peace, but energy. Though closer friends were bowed with grief, Sage felt unaccountably inspired and elated, almost like laughing. Perhaps someday, with the aid of his pure intentions and No-Name Stupid, he could approach the level of this man.

Ruby interrupted his reverie. "So, what exactly are you doing out here?" she asked. "Do you talk to people?"

"I've talked to some people,' said Sage. "I talked to one guy who said I'd find what I was looking for if I just kept knocking. And I met a crazy guy who looked like a frozen fish. I warmed him up by the campfire. He's pretty interesting, but he's crazy. He invents things." Sage shuddered.

"So, what's your name?" asked Ruby conversationally. "I'm Ruby Echevarria."

Sage never answered this question. Not in person. Not where anybody could see him. "I'm Halycon Sage," he said.

"I WONDER WHATEVER happened to Officer Sunshine," mused Halycon Sage a little later, over his third can of beer. They were drinking the real stuff now. "Did he do it again, or was once enough?"

"Do what?" asked Ruby. "Who are you talking about?"

"Officer Sunshine," Sage repeated. "Out in L.A. That wasn't his *real* name. This happened around '68, with the hippies. They had urban legends back then, too, just didn't call 'em that. Officer Sunshine was a cop—an L.A. cop even—which made the whole thing even more amazing."

"Okay?" asked Ruby, raising her winged eyebrow.

"Well, in that time of hope and promise," declaimed Sage, gesturing with his arm for the edification of imaginary masses, "when we thought peace was just around the corner, the hippies called the police 'pigs,' but *you* know, in kind of a *friendly* way, without anger—all except the L.A. ones. *These* cops were actively hated." It was all coming back to him.

"Wasn't there some big scandal about L. A. cops faking evidence?" asked Ruby.

"Yup. That came out later: corruption, brutality, faking evidence. But way back then, all we knew was it was a really bad scene."

He paused, faintly disoriented. Had he witnessed these things for himself, or had some older person told him about them? But perhaps it didn't matter.

The coffee table was cramping his style. Sage nudged it aside and rose to his feet, lecturing to an imaginary audience. This teaching style seemed very familiar.

"Then into this community/police disaster, this powder keg of rage, misunderstanding and mutual negative stereotyping, walked the great figure of Officer Sunshine. He was about to arrest some folks for dropping acid when somebody sarcastically handed him a tab of Orange Sunshine. This offer precipitated a satori-like awakening, a Moment of Truth."

His voice fell as the drama overcame him. "It suddenly occurred to him that he should not arrest people without understanding what they were doing and whether or not it was really wrong."

Ruby smiled. The common sense impressed her. She was liking Officer Sunshine.

"So, to the delight of everyone present," continued Sage, "he took the little tablet right there in broad daylight on the capitol steps and spend the next few hours in a state of melted bliss, looked after by his new-found friends. 'Officer Sunshine! Officer Sunshine!' they cried. And so it was." He bowed to his imaginary audience and resumed his seat on the couch.

Ruby popped another beer. "And you don't know what happened to him?"

"No, I've often wondered. Was he fired, did he go to prison, or what? And if he did, did he retain his awesome integrity? It would be interesting to meet him sometime. Maybe I could put him in one of my books."

This reminded Ruby of a bone she had to pick with Halycon Sage. "Why don't you ever put *women* in your books?"

"There's *nobody* in my books," said Sage. "They're too short."

"Then write longer ones," said Ruby, smacking him on the head with a pillow.

"I don't know any women," whined Halycon Sage.

"Then get to know some," said Ruby, shoving him back on the couch and planting a kiss on the surprised Halycon Sage with her red, red lips.

RUBY WAS SLEEPING in the bed, and Sage was staring at the crumpled pages of his growing autobiography.

He continued to write:

> And where and when, Dear Reader, did the denizens of the Dirty Dog *sleep*, known only to themselves? And why did they spend all day, sweet spring mornings, lazy summer afternoons, and invigorating autumn mid-days, in a dark, dark bar? And why was Ruby's skin so white, and her hair and eyes so black, and her lips so very, very red? And why were her polished fingernails so long? Was it only to frighten possible attackers? And why was Wolf named Wolf, and why were his long, long, hair and grizzled beard so very, very thick? Oh, surely, surely not. Oh surely this isn't *that* sort of book! There has been no hint, no foreshadowing at all. Oh, surely not. But yes, Dear Reader, yes—it is that sort of book . . .

He put down his pen. He couldn't do this. He couldn't do it to himself, and he couldn't do it to Ruby, sleeping peacefully beside him, her face a dusky gold in the morning light, not white at all. He didn't need to be a horror writer. There was enough horror in the world without him adding any more. Maybe he really *would* write a book about cows. You saw them often in the west, peaceful cows grazing in the wide green fields, standing still in sun and dappled shade, or moving slowly, gathering together under trees to shelter from the heat, feeling the perfumed wind and occasional rain. Beautiful animals, calm and gentle. Until one day—more horror.

Oh, well, it was a good life while it lasted. Something got us all in the end, cows or humans. Hopefully the end would be quick, or noble, or something. Maybe he'd just go back to *Boo Radley Goes Hawaiian*.

ONE THING ABOUT Sage really *was* Indian: he moved noiselessly. Nobody ever heard him coming or going unless he wanted them to. And he never told anybody where he was or what he was doing, so he did not tell Ruby when he left in the first light of dawn.

He stopped a moment, taking a long look at her peaceful face. He would see her again, he was sure. She was part of his fate. And then he did something alien to his nature, something akin to a high desert cloud coming down and saying hello. He took out his notebook and his special pen, and he wrote Ruby a note.

Because he was Halycon Sage, the note did not say where he was going or when he would be back, or even that he knew he would see her again. The note said, "I love you." Halycon Sage was a romantic, and he believed in the old things.

RUBY WASN'T PARTICULARLY surprised to wake and find Halycon Sage gone. She knew a lot about him, since he was her favorite author. She knew that he was the original Invisible Man: Nobody knew what he looked like or what state he lived in or even what his voice really sounded like. Nobody knew his age or his heredity, only that there was some mystery about it. Nobody knew when or where or how often he came and went.

What really surprised her was that he had revealed so much to her, that he had let her see his face, had told her his name, had spent a glorious, never-to-be-forgotten night with her in which they shared the depths of body, mind, and spirit. They had talked long into the night. She had told him all about the Dirty Dog gang and her love of motorcycles and reading, and he had shared something of the puzzles and confusions behind his slim, elegant books.

The other thing that surprised her was that he had left No-Name Stupid. This was fine with Stupid, who had liked and trusted Ruby from the moment she landed lightly on his back. He'd been tiring of Halycon Sage anyway, considering him muddle-headed and pretentious. And it was fine with Ruby. Taken together with the note, it seemed to her a token of supreme trust, reaffirming their permanent connection, even in the face of his leaving.

Ruby stepped to the mirror, smoothing back her hair in readiness for departure. She spoke to her reflection, as she sometimes did in thoughtful moments when she had something to say that could be shared with no one else.

"I love you, Halycon Sage," said Ruby. "I love you." She paused. "And I'm going to find you no matter how long it takes, and if you can't straighten yourself out, I am going to straighten you out myself." Then, thinking this sounded a little harsh and meddling, offering to take charge of someone's destiny on the strength of a single night, she added, "Or at least I'm coming along for the ride."

"Come on, horse," said Ruby, stepping outside into the sunlight where Stupid, for once, was tethered. "We've got things to do and people to see. No matter how long it takes." Stupid was acquiescent. He knew they were going to find Halycon Sage and deep down, no matter how annoyed he might be with his former companion, he was glad.

CHAPTER
NINE

BDURRAHEEM AND LAYLA sat by the side of the road with their suitcases, having nowhere else to go. Little Nuri played beside them. It was alright for *him*; he thought it was a vacation.

"Terrorists—they make me sick! I spit on them," said Abdurraheem, spitting into the gutter. "Al-Qaeda, Homeland Security, they make me sick." He spat again. "Politicians all sides, Tea Party, airport surveillance strip-search crazy nonsense, they make me sick," he added, spitting for a third, fourth and fifth time. He was not usually so bad mannered, but the aggravations of a lifetime had reached a crescendo and he was out of patience.

"Why do you let everybody make you sick?" asked Layla calmly. It was alright for her, too. She was very religious, and so was completely out of touch with reality—not like him, a practical person. "And stop that—you will run out of spit."

He spat one more time for *Daesh* (sometimes miscalled ISIS), a group so horrible that even al-Qaeda was disgusted and told them to knock it off. But it was true that his mouth was becoming exceedingly dry.

Abdurraheem was a nice man for whom everything had gone wrong. In fact, Halycon Sage's third novel might have been written especially for him. (Remember? "*A man went forth and he did everything right. But everything went wrong anyway. The End.*")

Born into the teaming confusion of a large, affectionate but somewhat suffocating Iraqi family, he had been drawn to the West. Unlike his many brothers and cousins, he longed for privacy: clean, quiet hotel rooms and other odd things. Of course he loved his family, but his mother's voice could cut wood, and he was sick of living in what he thought of somewhat guiltily as a mud hut. (Only a teenager could have characterized the large, gracious adobe structure in such a dismissive way.) He wanted to go to America, and with hard work, planning, scheming, networking, and the influence of a couple of brothers-in-law, he had done just that.

He could have entered any one of a number of professions and everything would have been fine. Banking, fine. Real estate or carpets or chain grocery stores, fine. Unfortunately, in college, like thousands of boys and girls before him, he had become air-struck.

Yes, Muhammad Abdurraheem Hussein, deciding on his course work in the 1990's, had fallen in love with planes and flying, with the beautiful uniforms and the adventure, the respect and the freedom. He fell in love with the technology and the flashing silver planes and the supersonic speeds and the white, gray, or golden clouds. With the storms and the radar and everything else about pilots and flying and planes. So, he elected to become an airline pilot.

For most young people this desire is an empty dream, possibly soon forgotten. For Abdurraheem, with perfect health and vision, lightening reflexes, straight A's, influence and money, it became a reality. He passed with flying colors and embarked on his career. Lucky him.

It was even worse. If flying was his life's work, he also had a hobby. He was an avid, enthusiastic gardener. In the courtyard of his family home were beautiful trees and flowers: lemon trees and grape vines, bougainvillea and hibiscus. Of course, he tried to replicate this idyllic background in his California garden.

As a practical, modern man, he had no patience with the organic movement. He wanted up-to-date things, things that worked. He hadn't clawed his way up the ladder of success to become some kind of hippie. So, unlike his more ecologically minded neighbors, he bought plenty of chemical fertilizer, which he stored in his garage.

To add to all this, he had terrible allergies. His wife insisted on keeping a cat, and Nuri would not be parted from the creature. The Prophet Muhammad had loved cats, peace and blessing be upon him, but Abdurraheem could only sneeze. And of course the cat, knowing this, contrived to wipe itself all over him at every opportunity, shedding the maximum amount of hair. Thus Abdurraheem also had a large supply of pseudoephedrine. He was not a man who bought a half-ounce of this and a capful of that. He believed in being prepared and keeping large supplies of anything he might need ready to hand.

And so it was that, after September of 2001, Abdurraheem became of a person of interest to the police, both local and national. He was the man who had everything. His first name identified him as a Muslim to everyone including Lutheran corn-growers from Iowa. His last name was shared with a crazy dictator. (In vain had he pointed out that "Hussein" was similar to "Smith" in the Muslim world.) He was a pilot. His garage was full of a prime bomb-making ingredient, his beloved chemical fertilizer, and his closet was full of the main ingredient for methamphetamine. To cap the whole thing off, he had an olive complexion and vivid, dark eyes, which glowed with the intensity of his determination to succeed in life.

About three quarters of the way down his long, slow slide from a respected citizen with a glamorous job to an unemployed nobody who was losing his house, he participated in some evaluation for job retraining. His caseworker was speechless. She was new, and not as tactful as she might have been. Upon first meeting her new client, in response to his plaintive question as to why no one would hire him, she had blurted out, "Because you look like a terrorist!" Her supervisor had had serious words with her, but the damage was done. Muhammad Abdurraheem Hussein was a bitter man.

Since even the best of us can be felled by the shifting winds of history and coincidence, please pity this unfortunate fellow—well-meaning and hard-working, but drawn to the wrong things, in the wrong place, at the wrong time.

Making a half-hearted attempt to get comfortable, Abdurraheem adjusted his legs in the dust of the road, leaned back against the cat carrier, and gave forth a mighty sneeze.

CHAPTER
TEN

**ANY MILES AWAY,** Halycon Sage was also sitting by a roadside. He was writing:

Like a madman, I throw myself against the padded walls.
Like a tiger, I throw myself against the bars of the cage.
Like a goldfish in a bowl, I go round and round
Meeting glass
Meeting glass
Invisible barriers all around . . .

I will be free, wrote Halycon Sage. I will be free.

Little did he know that just a few days before, No-Name Stupid had been thinking the very same thing.

Before setting out on his final, ultimate journey, Halycon Sage had one more piece of unfinished business to complete. (It might be posited that, like someone perpetually falling in love, Sage was always convinced that *this* time was the Real Thing.) A bus ride over dusty land, a short walk down a small, shady street and he stood before the door of a white house with peeling paint. The Indian Ancestry Office.

Halycon Sage walked in, scuffing his boot on the floor in sudden shyness. This meant so much to him.

"Do you have my results?" he asked the receptionist. "I'm the one who called this morning."

The large woman behind the desk looked at him impassively.

"Yes, Mr. Vasselschnauzer," she said, trying to match the strange name with the man in front of her and not succeeding. "We've completed your DNA test."

"Well?" asked the false Vasselschnauzer, shyness giving way to impatience. "Please tell me. What tribe am I? What state do they come from? Do you have a town or a village for me? Your ads said you could pinpoint ancestry very specifically."

"Well, *pretty* specifically," said the woman. "*Relatively* specifically. You can't expect the world for one-hundred-and-twenty-nine bucks."

This was definitely a low-rent operation. He could have afforded much better, a thousand times better, but he had grown up in poverty and could never drop the mindset. "Please tell me," he repeated urgently. He had waited so long to find out. "What am I?"

"Give me the money first," said the woman. He handed her one-hundred-and-twenty-nine dollars, folded carefully together.

The woman put it away and made a notation in a little book. She wrote out a receipt and handed it to him.

"According to our precise, scientific calculations, your heritage is probably from New Mexico, or Arizona. Or maybe the northern part of Mexico. Or Nevada. There was a lot of intermarriage of tribes in that area, so science has not yet been able to distinguish the precise tribe with any accuracy."

She looked at him critically, squinting a little with one eye. "But me, from my personal experience, I'd say you were maybe Apache, or Mescalero. Or Zapotec, or Aztec. Or maybe from further north, maybe Arapaho or Navajo. Some kind of ho, anyway."

"Thanks a bunch," said Halycon Sage, and got back to saving the world.

SAGE AWOKE WITH a start. It was the same dream again. He glanced around the little clearing that held his makeshift campsite, then lay back in his sleeping bag, listening to the rustling leaves and breathing deeply as he contemplated the strange, recurring dream.

The country dark, darker than any city ever was, punctuated by a million diamond stars. Faint shadows of trees. Flickering firelight. A strange absence: the electric hum of refrigerators, generators, power lines. The constant undertone of electricity . . . was gone.

The rocks glowed red. Intense heat; yet deeper blackness. Bodies close around him. The beauty of chanting voices and hearts' desires simply spoken. The smell of grass, water, trees, wind, smoke.

After the ceremony, alone outside with the old man, the leader. The old man was nothing much to look at—jeans, plaid shirt, hair cut short. They sat on two big rocks, looking at each other. Their stillness was not forced, not strained, not even expectant. They sat and looked. And at last the old man nodded. He saw Halycon Sage and knew him to the core. Yes, said the old man silently, in response to the being, the quest, and the heart of Halycon Sage. Yes.

He lay there a little longer, mulling over the dream and some other fragmented memories. It was probably illegal to sleep where he'd been sleeping, so he'd better be moving on soon. But it was so comfortable just resting and thinking.

He was traveling on foot now, staying away from motels, towns, and people. Trying to think clearly, trying to remember a past that was sometimes a confusing blur, a scatter of fallen leaves, unconnected and blown every which way. He was coming reluctantly to a certain conclusion: to save the world, a technological solution was needed.

This conclusion went against all his instincts and desires. He wanted to talk to people, convince them with human contact, not manipulate them with impersonal machines. He wanted to use reason, philosophy, psychology, even prayer. He wanted to use insight, and the music of words, to get them to stop killing each other and abusing the animals and destroying the earth. He wanted them to use their money and energy and intelligence to find solutions, instead of using them against each other.

In his former life, before he was Halycon Sage, he had done this. He had written essays and articles, short stories and poems and editorials. He had taught classes. He had read anything that might provide a clue. He had attended meetings and organized them, had participated in campaigns and rallies and demonstrations and marches.

And he had prayed with everybody. For Halycon Sage, the Way of the Cross and the Way of the Pipe, the Six-Pointed Star and the Star and Crescent, the Dharma Wheel and all the others, they all led to the same place. It was a good Place, the Only Place—he *knew* that, he had seen and felt it.

But with all this, he couldn't be reconciled, because there was still the mindless slaughter. The greed and stupidity and cruelty went on and on, with innocent people and animals crushed in its unclean jaws, and Halycon Sage could not resign himself to it. No spiritual state or philosophical insight could make it bearable . . .

A whirr of wings, and he turned his head toward the sound. Like the old man in the dream, the hummingbird was saying yes. It hovered beside his ear, affirming his thoughts, confirming his direction.

His mind returned to the vague cascade of years: marches and rallies, workshops and articles, prayers and ceremonies. Except for a few highlights, this was all he remembered of his former life as the most minor and forgettable of writers. It was only after his rebirth as Halycon Sage that the public had come to accept him. The meteoric rise of his silly minimalist novels was a phenomenon paralleling the worldwide acceptance of the Happy Day Face. Who knows why anything catches on? *He* certainly didn't.

If the critics had read his thoughts in these moments, they would have been elated, for here at last was the key to the mystery of Halycon Sage. Who was he really? And why was it that the most intrepid investigation could not trace his background? Why, since his emergence from nothing and nowhere into the spotlight of worldwide fame, was he absolutely unwilling to discuss his parentage, his upbringing, his family, his education, or anything to do with his past? Why was he unwilling to answer the simplest stock questions of the kind asked by interviewers of authors: When did you decide to become a writer? Where were you born? Did you have sisters and brothers? What was it like for you growing up, and how did that influence your work? Were you rich or poor? *Are* you Native American? Are you full-blooded? What tribe are you from? And on and on.

Halycon Sage pretended he wouldn't answer these questions because he was an eccentric, a writer with interesting, writerly quirks. His editor liked it. It gave him a caché and increased what she liked to call his "mystique." It was one of the reasons for his phenomenal success.

But the truth was, he didn't answer the questions because he, just like the readers and interviewers and critics, had no freaking idea what most of the answers *were*. He remembered only the vaguest outline of the things he had done, and that his struggle against the machine of dehumanization had been lifelong. For Halycon Sage, of course, had amnesia.

HE HAD WOKEN one morning in an alley, concussed and bleeding, money and identification gone. He wore blue jeans and a tee shirt, dusty boots and longish hair. He had no idea who he was or how he had gotten there.

He found a nearby gas station and staggered into the bathroom, watched by the suspicious clerk who had reluctantly given him the key. He looked in the mirror and saw that he was an Indian. An Indian who had apparently been in a fight. A disreputable spectacle.

For even this basic piece of ethnic data—that he was Native American—he had had to look outside himself. He remembered almost nothing. He knew that he was a man and a writer, that he fought for truth against lies, and that both the lies and the truth took many forms. And he remembered an address. But that was all.

He bathed his face in the blessedly cool water, washing away the dust and dirt and traces of blood. There was a small black comb in his pocket, his only remaining possession besides his clothes. As he combed his hair, some words echoed in his ears, part of his last dream before waking. "*One Hundred and One Cows: A Novel.*" He had no idea what they meant.

With his hair combed and face washed, brushing the dust from his clothes, he saw that he was not a bad-looking man, and tall. Good—this could come in handy. After all, nobody wanted to be ugly. The bruises were less noticeable than he had first thought. Most of them had been merely dirt, and the cuts on the side of his head from which the blood had run were hidden in his hair. He walked out of the bathroom.

"I'd like to use your phone, please," he told the clerk, and was relieved to see her hostility fade. "I'll need to call a taxi."

The clerk blushed a little, dropping her eyes and reaching for a telephone. "Sorry about before, sir," she said. "We get some odd types in here, and you have to be careful."

"No problem," said the nameless man who would become Halycon Sage. They chatted companionably while he waited for his cab. They opened a package of Fritos (on the house), while she told him of the difficulties of raising children single-handed on a clerk's salary. Her name was Margie.

As the taxi rolled quietly toward the city center, the Somalian driver was charmed to see that this Native American man could speak Somali. And Arabic as well, apparently.

"*Sabah wanaagsan*," said the nameless man, since it was morning. "*Khaif halak?*" he added, inquiring after the driver's health and wellbeing. He had given the only address he knew, 422 W. Broadway. He had some idea he should be in the Southwest, but this looked like Manhattan, and Broadway was *in* Manhattan. He smiled to himself, pleased that he knew these geographical details. He knew a suite number, too, but he was keeping that to himself for now.

The taxi purred along, moving deeper into the city. It stopped in front of a tall building. "*Ma salaama,*" the passenger told the driver. Go in peace. The driver was charmed, but not charmed enough to work for nothing. "Hey, what about my fare?" he asked.

"Sorry," said the passenger. "I guess I got too involved in our discussion. I'll be right back." Shutting the door, he strode purposefully toward the majestic gold and white entrance of the tall building.

This behavior was not to be tolerated, but the driver sat strangely still, wondering uneasily if he'd been conned. There was something about the man, something that made you want to believe him and help him. It wasn't just his linguistic abilities.

The man who would be Sage pushed a golden button and stepped into one of a bank of elevators. He smiled slightly, and the passengers smiled and made room for him.

Remember, Dear Reader, that he was amnesiac, concussed and not quite in his right mind. If he had been, perhaps he would not have acted as he did, but everything was flowing naturally, as in a dream, with a sort of inevitability. He opened the door to Suite 1403 and walked in. He didn't bother with the empty reception desk but walked straight down the line of offices to a door marked Kathryn McCready. The name seemed familiar somehow.

As he stepped in, a neat, black-haired woman looked up inquiringly.

"I'm ... " he said, and stopped. It occurred to him that he had no name. There was a bunch of sage on the desk in a little, Hopi-made pot. A real one by the look of it. The sage seemed familiar and touched his heart.

"I'm Halycon Sage, the writer," he said. "You're publishing my books."

Ms. McCready could not recall his name offhand. Unlike some publishers in these troubled times, her company had many authors. Most she had never met. "Oh, certainly," she said smoothly. "I'll just pull your file." She slid her chair toward the large, forest-green filing cabinet.

"I have a taxi waiting," said the new Halycon Sage. "I have to pay him."

Without a word, the editor handed him three fifties. Who knew what his taxi was charging? He didn't have any luggage, apparently. She sighed. These writers were so impractical. He had probably made no reservations either, and would want to stay with her. It had happened before.

Halycon Sage traversed his previous route, paid the driver, added a generous tip and returned to the editor's office. She couldn't find his file, which intrigued her, since she never lost anything. But she was almost sure now that she had heard his name. It had a certain resonance. She settled him comfortably in a black leather chair with a cup of coffee—cream and sugar.

"I suppose we'd better talk," said Halycon Sage.

HE SAT UP in his sleeping bag, sweeping the hair out of his eyes and dismissing all these dreams and memories. Though more had come back to him over time, it wasn't enough to bother with, especially since he still had his mission to complete. He hadn't even started, really.

Having come to the unpalatable conclusion that a technological solution was needed, he knew himself to be far outside his areas of expertise. He rose from the ground with something between a grunt and a sigh, and re-rolled his sleeping bag. There was no getting around it. Like it or not, he would have to find Alexander Preisczech.

NOT SO FAR away, Preisczech had come to a similar conclusion: He had to find Halycon Sage. The decision had followed him into his dreams. "I need him. I need him. He sees the things I *don't see*. I need him. I need him. He sees the things I *don't see*." Preisczech was mumbling rhythmically in his sleep. It was almost a chant. He woke with a start.

"Halycon Sage, *where are you*?" he cried from the depths of his soul.

"Shaddup, ya moron," came the response from down the hall. It was true, what his parents had told him. To every question, there was always an answer.

CHAPTER

ELEVEN

 **THROUGH SOME MIRACLE** of synchronicity, everyone was looking for everyone else, some on the internet, some through other means.

Halycon Sage was looking for Preisczech, while Preisczech was looking for Halycon Sage. Wolf, along with Ratbone from the Fifth Street Mofos, was looking for Ruby. Drake and Muldoon, having lost track of the mysterious foreigner, were looking for more traces of Project Lazlex, and Basel Vasselschnauzer was looking for Halycon Sage. Ruby and No-Name Stupid were also looking for Halycon Sage.

Josh was simultaneously reading a *Thor the Dentist* comic and looking for a hot date online, hoping the librarian wouldn't walk by. Trevor, more serious, was looking for "Lazlex," trying to make sure his soon-to-be-patented computer game did not duplicate the name of some tampon or nasal spray.

The boys were in the library because, according to Trevor, they would be more focused working side by side and could complete this final step more quickly. Luckily for Josh, Trevor was *too* focused to notice what Josh had up on his screen.

Sophie, Josh's brilliant sister who went to the same school as Josh and Trevor, was looking online for the *Maitreya Buddha*, the Buddha Who Was to Come, while Layla, wife of the much-tested Abdurraheem Hussein, was looking online for the *Mahdi, another* savior who was to come. Both had come to the conclusion that everything was so awful it *must* be the end of the world. Brother Bob Hoskins, formerly of the Free-Swinging Evangelical Church, had completely slipped his trolley and was looking online for the Antichrist. Mossad and MI6 were tracking Preisczech, while Homeland Security and al-Qaeda were tracking Halycon Sage.

Editor Kathryn McCready was looking for Halycon Sage because the serial rights to *Boo Radley Goes Hawaiian* had been sold and drafts of the first three chapters were due. Hamden McPete was looking for Halycon Sage because, since Sage's disappearance, he feared that his negative review had sent the sensitive author over the edge. Several species and varieties of bill collector were also looking for Halycon Sage.

At the moment, Halycon Sage was sitting in a bar, a medium-sized one with tacky, red-flocked cathouse wallpaper where there wasn't dark old paneling. He was not drinking; he was talking to people.

Nobody had found anybody yet, but everyone was giving it their best.

 OBODY WAS LOOKING for Basel Vasselschnauzer— everyone was glad he was gone.

The secret vice of Basel Vasselschnauzer was that he was extremely lazy. He wanted to do absolutely nothing, while living off the fat of the land and being admired by all.

This feat is much more easily accomplished by the rich than by the poor, and Basel Vasselschnauzer, before he had been sent out to find Halycon Sage, had almost achieved it. He had an unobtrusive French chef who made his meals appear as if by magic. Cleaning was also done invisibly. He had a special room, done in shades of deep blue and taupe, for viewing the arty films he sometimes reviewed. He had another room, done in olive green and peach, where he pretended to read the books sent him by publishers and where he wrote his razor-sharp reviews. When out and about, he sat around in bars and cafes, drinking the latest fashionable drink, eating lobster and caviar, chatting with his friends and enemies. The price of caviar had gone through the roof, but it was essential to his self-image that he be seen consuming it.

Nobody admired him exactly, but almost everyone feared him. And he did nothing but write one small syndicated weekly column, which he accomplished with a great deal of complaining.

WHO IS HALYCON *Sage*??? Why, only the most revered post-modernist minimalist pseudo-realist neo-symbolist writer alive, the founder of the whole *school* of post-modern minimalist neosymbolic pseudo-realism, *that's all*! But don't feel bad if you've never heard of him. There are two guys in the Kalahari Desert who haven't heard of him either, so at least you're not alone!"

From psychoblogger at:
www.halyconsagefest. com

PREISCZECH WAS IN a quandary. He had tried everything to find Halycon Sage. He'd gone back on foot, by bus and by thumb to all the places they had frequented. (Being from Europe, he didn't know how dangerous it was to hitchhike in the USA.) He'd talked to everyone, and there was nothing. Sage had truly lived up to his nickname, the Invisible Man. Only one old man, the proprietor of a run-down motel, had said he'd seen No-Name Stupid being ridden away by a beautiful, black-haired woman. But this made no sense. Halycon Sage didn't know any women and would certainly never have parted with Stupid. Finding the real world disappointing, Preisczech had turned to the internet.

He found volumes of information on Halycon Sage, more than he had ever wanted to know. He discovered that his simple friend was known, picked over, and analyzed around the world. There were online discussion groups and fan clubs, chat rooms and much hot debate. There was even talk of a Halycon Sage *festival.* But there was nothing remotely believable about either his background or his whereabouts. (Preisczech discounted the space alien story.)

At this point in his endeavors, having reached a certain level of desperation, Preisczech decided to post his *own* message in the hope that Sage would find it. He had a sort of intuition that Sage was seeking him as well. They had been so good together, two eccentric geniuses whose minds fit like puzzle pieces, each filling in the appalling blind spots of the other.

But this was his dilemma: Preisczech wanted to find Halycon Sage, but he didn't want any government agencies to find *him.* Things had taken a turn for the better in his life, at least in the area of government surveillance. He had been to the same supermarket four times in the past three weeks, and nobody had screamed, "Preisczech!" at him. He had begun to believe his ordeal was over. The last thing he wanted to do was stir the whole thing up again. So, he couldn't put his real name on the internet.

He had to be clever, canny, like the spies in the movies. He had to think the way they did: find a code word, something secret, something only Halycon Sage would understand. He thought and thought, pounding his head gently and rhythmically with his fist.

And then it came to him: LAZLEX. This special name was known only to the two of them. The Dirty Dog gang had heard it once, but they were no threat. They had been much too impaired to remember. Yet because of their drunken laughter, so painful at the time but suddenly revealed as fortuitous, Preisczech had never told the name to another living soul. Except for Halycon Sage.

Working quickly, Preisczech set up a LAZLEX site. Anyone besides Sage who showed up could be fobbed off with some excuse. He thought a moment about what that might be. Aha! "Lazlex" could be explained as a new fabric that didn't wrinkle in the drier, or maybe an ecologically friendly fiber made of cornhusks—something so boring no one would pursue it. But presumably no one but Halycon Sage would respond anyway.

Preisczech established a Facebook Fan Page describing the amazing miracle fiber, Lazlex. Then he wrote one message on the status wall: "Halycon Sage. Please come back. I want you. I need you. Meet me at that last motel where we stayed." Wanting to break through the coldness of the internet medium, to emphasize the urgency of his request, he added, "We were so good together!"

Preisczech's English had remained spotty and eccentric, though his vocabulary had improved considerably. He did not realize that his message sounded like a cheap romance novel. His mind was only on science, on finding Sage to help him see what he was missing, something Sage always did so well. He was focused entirely on unleashing his latest grotesque invention—God help us all!—the nanobots.

CHAPTER
TWELVE

**N AN INTERNET** cafe, Basel Vasselschnauzer was working on his column. He was typing with one finger because he was bored. He could do this faster than most people could type with both hands. When he used all *ten* fingers they moved like the wind. Speed typing and dart throwing were his only useful accomplishments other than knowing everything about everybody (with one important exception) and cutting people to ribbons with his words.

Having plowed through the voluminous list of his Dislikes, he had moved on to his Likes. "WE LIKE BLUE VELVET," he wrote. "And green satin. They'll be really big this fall. WE LIKE top hats, and young ladies and gentlemen with manners. You'll be seeing a resurgence of those, too. WE LIKE hydrangeas, but only the blue ones, so if you're a gardener, don't forget to adjust the soil."

And then he wrote, as he had written so many weeks before, "WE LIKE HALYCON SAGE. WE, BASEL VASSELSCHNAUZER, WILL FIND HIM. WE ARE HOT ON THE TRAIL."

Glancing down at the high-end omelet that had just arrived, he ended his column. "And WE LIKE MUSHROOMS. Especially MORELS. Someone send a case of them to US immediately, care of the editor." "FROZEN," he added, not being sure when he would return. But when he did, the mushrooms would be there. He had done things like this before, and the readers always came through.

WOLF AND RATBONE sat in the bar, staring at Ratbone's battered old laptop. After a fruitless search of the neighborhood for Ruby, Wolf had suggested looking for Halycon Sage, her favorite author, online. Ruby was normally a woman of few words, but she couldn't shut *up* about this pretentious clown once she got started. She had once or twice mentioned trying to find him. So, if Wolf found Halycon Sage, he might find Ruby. He was desperate enough to try anything, and how hard could it be? After all, the guy was world famous.

"I be steady tellin' you," said Ratbone, tapping keys, "they ain't nothin' nowhere about the whereabouts of no Halycon Sage. Literary criticism, yes. Fan clubs, yes. Festival, yes. Whereabouts, no. Lest you believe that story about the Mothership. Because I done *looked*."

"But, dude," said Wolf. "There's gotta be. *Everything's* on the internet, man."

"It's true, can't nobody keep no secrets no more," said Ratbone, flashing his gold tooth. "Even the gov'ment can't keep no secrets. Even the Communists. But this Sage, man, he ain't *on* the internet. All *about* him, yes, but he *hisself ain't on it.* He don't never go there, is what I think."

"Aw, man, give it one more try," pleaded Wolf. "*Everybody* goes on the internet—it's only natural. And you're the best dude for knowin' the ins and outs of it," he continued, trying flattery. "C'mon, Ruby's like my *sister*, man. I *gotta* get her back!"

"That Ruby's tough," said Ratbone. "She ain't about to get lost lessen she *want* to get lost." He sighed, giving way momentarily to Wolf's pleading puppy-eyes. "Okay, I try one more time, but that is *all*."

WHAT'S THIS?" ASKED Muldoon, suddenly sitting up. He had been sliding lower and lower in his chair all afternoon. "*This* wasn't here before!"

Drake let out a little snore. There was white donut powder all over his shirtfront. *He's a cartoon, but he's my partner,* thought Muldoon. "Drake! Wake up! I found something!"

"*Halycon Sage. Please come back,*" read Drake, rubbing his bleary eyes. "*I want you. I need you. Meet me at that last motel where we stayed. We were so good together*!" "What's this crap? You woke me up for this?"

"Yeah, but look at the title," said Muldoon.

"I be go to hell," said Drake, finally waking up. "It's Lazlex."

THIS WASN'T HERE before," announced Ratbone, suddenly straightening in his chair. "I thought we done looked at all twenty-seven million, five thousand three hundred and sixty-five Halycon Sage entries, but this is a new one. Must be twenty-seven million, five thousand three hundred and sixty-*six*.

"*Halycon Sage,*" he read. "*I want you. I need you.* Oh, man, I gotta answer this one. I gotta have *some* fun all up in this sorry-ass bar."

Wolf shook his head, resigned. So, Ratbone typed the first answer to Preisczech's heartfelt plea. "Oh, baby!" He paused for a moment. "Oh, baby, baby, yeah! Oh, yeah, baby, I be Halycon Sage, and I be wantin' you, too. Just call me at," he thought a moment, filled in an area code, then typed a number at random. The number seemed musical somehow, and pleased him. "I be waitin', honey," his message continued. "I be waitin'."

Though this was the first message of this kind that Preisczech received, it was by no means the last. Some writers were more explicit than Ratbone who, after all, possessed a certain delicacy. It must have been a boring day on the internet, filled with people who needed to get a life. Either that, or the mere mention of Halycon Sage overrode everybody's inhibitions.

AMAZINGLY, JOSH FOUND the new posting before his partner did. There had been nothing about "Lazlex" before, yet here it was.

"Oh, that's just swell," said Trevor, who was trying to bring back old slang in his spare time. "A non-wrinkle fiber made entirely of corn husks. That you can make at home."

"Just send two boxtops," added Josh, from his own imagination. He was an aficionado of classic comic books and had always wanted to send two boxtops. "Who the frick is Halycon Sage?"

GOT IT!" SAID Hamden McPete to himself, as he found the new entry.

"Got it!" said Ms. Lydia Wentworth-Brewster, of MI6.

"Got it!" said Lev Goldstein of Mossad.

"Got it!" said Sean Raintree of the C.I.A.

"Got it!" said Abu Mu'awiya of al-Qaeda, diverted for a moment from the annoying damp of his computerized cave. The one damp cave in this whole miserable mountain range and of course *he* had gotten it.

"Hmmmm," said Kathryn McCready, "'Oh, baby, baby . . . ' This looks more current than the other stuff. Maybe this woman has seen him recently."

She had been reading manuscripts for ten hours and did not quite take in that the message was supposed to be *from* Halycon Sage.

"Oh, for Heaven's sake!" said Basel Vasselschnauzer, reading the message and discretely picking bits of omelet out of his teeth with a gold toothpick. "What *now*?"

ALYCON SAGE WAS going around in circles. Literally. He was on foot, spiraling round and round at the Sagebrush River Memorial Mystic Maze and Bottle Shop in an undisclosed western state. There was no alcohol in the bottle shop; the proprietor was not familiar with the original British expression and used his emporium instead to sell pretty bottles made of rare desert glass, made pale or deeper purple by the sun.

Sage had thought leaving Ruby and No-Name Stupid behind would leave him clearer, freer. (Or freeer? Free-er? He had left his thesaurus and dictionary behind as well.) Clearer and more free to pursue his destiny in a single-minded way, without distraction. But it had had no such effect. It had not even made his life quieter, since his internal dialogue was infinitely louder and more chaotic than the comparatively peaceful woman and horse. At the center of the maze, he paused. He lay down on the soft, green grass, looking up at the cool, blooming lilacs, the blue sky and the quickly drifting clouds. There was no sound but the wind. The smell of flowers and grass enveloped him. Silent tears rolled out of the corners of his eyes and slid into his ears, just as in the purportedly humorous country song.

"*What do you want, Halycon Sage?*" asked a kindly voice that seemed to come from everywhere and nowhere. "*What do you really, really want?*" He had not known the answer to this before, but now suddenly he knew.

The tears had stopped. He felt very calm. "I just want to be home," he said quietly. "Wherever I belong. Where there are people like me. That's all I've ever wanted." He waited, at peace, since he had finally found his heart's desire and communicated it to someone, possibly a Wise Being.

There was a timeless pause. The sweet scents drifted and the wind sighed. After a timeless interval, the voice spoke again.

"*But you see,*" said the voice kindly, "*you don't belong anywhere. And I'm afraid there isn't really anybody else like you, Halycon Sage.*"

Halycon Sage sat up. "Thanks," he said. "I needed that."

"*Of course you did,*" said the voice. "*Have a nice day.*"

CHAPTER
THIRTEEN

BASEL **V**ASSELSCHNAUZER **WANTED** to go home. He was tired of the grubby motel in the south-western city, tired of sitting in unfamiliar restaurants and bars as he traveled the wastelands beyond New Jersey, tired of talking to people who were neither friends nor enemies. And he had a small blister on his little toe. Such a thing had never happened before. Surely this above all demonstrated the sincerity and longevity of his effort to find Halycon Sage. Surely no more could be asked of any civilized man.

Quickly he typed his message onto the Lazlex site: "HALYCON SAGE IS WITH ME. I have him here, and he's not leaving, ever, because he realizes that I am the cleverest, most talented man in the world and I AM HIS BEST FRIEND."

Being reasonably sure that Halycon Sage loathed him, he counted on outrage to bring the author to his door—or at least to his telephone or computer. After signing his name to this message, he added his room number and the address of his motel. It looked a little plain somehow, not interesting enough. On impulse he typed above the address: "Project Lazlex Regional Headquarters."

Then he pressed "Send" and sat back with a sigh. Now all he had to do was wait. If the message did not bring Sage to his door, it would certainly bring someone close to Sage who would know his location. From his long experience of the literary world, the critic knew one thing for sure: people will always leap forward to repudiate an obvious lie. If you say someone is where they are not, doing something they have never thought of, that individual will contact you instantly and never stop bothering you until they get a retraction. (Not that anybody ever got any change out of Basel Vasselschnauzer. He retired to the Riviera on such occasions.)

Basel Vasselschnauzer had lived so long divorced from the real world, surrounded by toadying flatterers, snide but impotent enemies, and omnipresent, invisible servants, that he had no idea such a course of action might be dangerous.

OF COURSE ALMOST everyone tracking the Lazlex site read Vasselschnauzer's message. Within a couple of hours, most of the web surfers were converging by car, bus or airplane (according to their budgets) on the specified location. A less active but equally intrepid minority was persistently trying to track down Ratbone's fake telephone number, but the results seemed entirely irrelevant. For the older and less computer literate searchers, there was something strange about that number. Very strange. Somehow you wanted to *hum* it.

Of all the people who had decided to question Basel Vasselschnauzer, it was pure luck that Josh and Trevor arrived first, closely followed by Hamden McPete, who was visiting the Southwest on a lecture tour. Josh and Trevor had no interest in Halycon Sage or Basel Vasselschnauzer, but they thought that since Lazlex Corp. was practically around the corner they might as well check it out.

Drake and Muldoon, also nearby, were amazed to find that their long-sought target was only about fifteen minutes away from their secret location. They should have been first on the scene, but by the time they got permission to leave the building, it had been several hours.

It just goes to show, thought Drake bitterly. *Anybody else would get a nice hotel stay and a plane ride with an expense account for meals and booze, but no, we gotta drive down an alley and take two left turns. Why does God hate me?*

Vasselschnauzer was oblivious to the whirlwind of chaos about to descend on his head. He was not street-smart enough to be worried about his message and the unsavory visitors it might bring, and he had no need to look further for Halycon Sage, having every expectation now that Halycon Sage would contact *him*. So, he had taken refuge in the pleasant routine of his ordinary work and was preparing to bat out an edition of WHAT WE LIKE AND WHY. He sifted through the pile of manuscripts he had brought along to sooth his feelings and channel his bad temper. Some of them had been sitting in his apartment for years. Other, newer ones he had brought for comedy relief, to amuse himself and send terse comments back to his editor for the adoring public. He picked up one of the latter, glancing at the name of the author.

"Niemand Kompt. NEE-mahnd COMB-T," said Basel Vasselschnauzer, spitting the ultimate "t" through his teeth. "Like pocket comb with a 't' on the end," he murmured to himself. An existentialist, he had heard. An up-and-coming writer. Already he didn't like this guy. There was something odd about the name . . . "Niemand Kompt, Niemand Kompt," he muttered to himself, scrambling for a translation, digging around in his centuries-old German. (At least it felt that way.

It was a long time since he had lobbed a spitwad so neatly at the German teacher's head. For all his effete ways, Vasselschnauzer's aim with the arm was as deadly as his aim with the pen.)

There was something *wrong* with that name. But what? "Niemand Kompt. Niemand Kompt," he repeated. Then it hit him. "*Niemand kommt—nobody's coming*!" he shouted in triumph, proud to have nabbed the elusive definition. "That's what it means: Nobody's coming."

"Well, *that's* cheerful," he mumbled sarcastically, continuing his out-loud monologue. He slammed his whiskey glass down on the cheap hotel coffee table. He was not a whiskey drinker, not normally. The cheap whiskey—his expense account was running low, gone were the days of champagne and caviar—sat upon the wobbly coffee table, which was covered in thin brown plywood, apparently stained with shoe polish. *Nice patina, goes with the rest of the décor*, he thought viciously. He had come down to this, and all because of Halycon Sage, whom he could not find, who would *never* be found. Sneaky so-and-so.

Vasselschnauzer removed his leather-slippered feet from the disgusting table and considered the manuscript in his hand. He had not deigned to write a whole column in weeks. They had a backlog they could use. And none of the dolts who read him would notice if they started rerunning the old ones. Already he was prepared to dislike this Niemand Kompt, to rip him into literary shreds. Still, Basel Vasselschnauzer was a fair man. He would treat this writer impartially, giving him the same objective trial he gave to all his authors.

"I love him, I love him not," muttered Vasselschnauzer, removing the hallowed dartboard from its customary place on the kitchen counter and hanging it on the back of the motel door. As usual, he made a little ritual of this. It was so important to establish his attitude toward a new author right away, especially one who looked like becoming popular with the public, sticking around for a while. Ceremoniously he drew out the two darts, the red-feathered dart of life, and the black-feathered dart of death. Whichever came closest to the bull's eye would set the tone. With a sneer on his face and eyes closed he threw them both, then sat down to write.

An hour later he hit the "Send" button on his laptop. It was perhaps slightly unfortunate that the last column Basel Vasselschnauzer would ever write, the very last appearance on this earth of WHAT WE LIKE AND WHY, would contain a vicious attack on the up-and-coming writer, Niemand Kompt. Because Niemand Kompt was crazy as a bedbug.

"WHAT KIND OF corporate headquarters is this?" asked Trevor, staring in disbelief at the rundown motel. "Geez, this is no threat. If *this* is all we have to worry about, we can just go ahead and patent the game. Don't even have to go in there, dude."

"Well, let's check it out anyway," said Josh, "as long as we're here." And he knocked.

'GO AWAY!!" shrieked Basel Vasselschnauzer, jolted out of his usual poisonous urbanity by the unprecedented circumstance of someone's knocking on his door. 'WE DON'T LIKE VISITORS! EVER!"

What the frick? thought Josh, knocking again. A small, bald-headed man appeared at his right shoulder. "Are you young men by any chance looking for Halycon Sage?" he asked in an unexpectedly deep and resonant voice. "Because he may have done himself an injury, and I'm rather afraid it's my fault. Have you any information?"

"No, sir," said Trevor politely. "We never heard of Halycon Sage until this morning. We're looking for Lazlex Corp. Who are you?"

"Hamden McPete, at your service. And this seems an unlikely location for either of them," he mused. "*Or* for Basel Vasselschnauzer, for that matter. He's a man who likes to do himself well. I can't see him staying *here*." He wondered if he had written down the wrong address. He was 97, after all, and getting a little absent-minded.

An unearthly silence issued from the motel room. The irascible columnist had finally grokked the implications of his situation. His current strategy was *not coming out*, ever. Unfortunately, the door was flimsy and the next two arrivals were more determined to make contact. Don't ask how Ms. Lydia Wentworth-Brewster of MI6 and Mr. Sean Raintree of the C.I.A. managed to get to the motel room so fast. Don't ask. Don't even think about it. They have their ways, and it's much better for you not to know. *Much* better.

The two arrived simultaneously from different directions and almost collided with each other. Neither was aware that the other group had the technology for this impossible, almost instantaneous trip. Recovering their poise, they took each other's measure. *Yes, one of us*, they thought.

"Top secret psychic research?" asked Raintree. "Out of body travel?"

"Hardly," said Ms. Wentworth-Brewster in her tidy English accent. "I wouldn't be holding *this* if I were in my astral body, now would I?" The gun was small but businesslike. "What about you? Atom displacement?"

"Can't talk about it," said Raintree. "Top Secret. Are you after Sage or Vasselschnauzer?"

"Preisczech, actually. You've heard of him?"

We just can't stay ahead of them, thought Raintree. *Sneaky English, how the hell do they know about Preisczech?* "He's the real target," he said, throwing caution to the winds. "If his latest invention gets away from us—"

"Civilization as we know it will be over," Ms. W-B finished for him, and with one accord they rushed the door, bruising their shoulders, firing shots in the direction of the lock, scattering bemused civilians Josh, Trevor, and McPete, and scaring the stuffing out of Basel Vasselschnauzer as they crashed into his room in a shower of wood dust and splinters.

A FEW MINUTES later, when McPete, Josh, and Trevor decided it was safe to come out—they had been hiding variously behind an enormous decorative clay jug and an inadequate palm tree—there was once again an unearthly silence. Stepping cautiously into the damaged motel room, they beheld a strange sight. Basel Vasselschnauzer was passed out cold, stunned senseless by the bravest and most proactive thing he had ever done.

He had been about to review a second manuscript, the demolition of Niemand Kompt having so soothed his nerves that he was prompted to repeat the experience. As the agents burst in, his lightening-like reflexes—so at odds with other aspects of his character—had been activated by his panic at seeing them and he had thrown both the red and the black darts toward the developing chaos coming from behind the door. The first one, the black, had hit Mr. Sean Raintree on the exact tip of the nose. It was thrown hard and it had hurt, but more than that, it had triggered a life-long fear carefully concealed by Mr. Raintree from his high-level superiors—the fear of blindness. Working as he did around bombs and bullets, this was the occupational hazard he feared more than death. (Human psychology is strange; we all have these little quirks.)

Ms. Lydia Wentworth-Brewster was also *hors du combat*, but for a different reason. As an agent, she was known to be cool, caustic, and unflappable even in the heat of battle. But somehow her *face* had never been threatened. One might have guessed from the unusual perfection of her hair, makeup, and clothing in all but the most desperate situations that her hidden flaw was *vanity*. When the red dart struck her, like her American counterpart, on the exact tip of the nose, lightening visions of scars, red marks, and plastic surgery sent her screaming to the bathroom mirror. She slammed the door behind her.

So Trevor and Josh were met with the spectacle of two men passed out on the floor, accompanied by a faint wailing from behind the bathroom door. This was not their idea of a boring agricultural corporation.

"I believe I will avail myself of the amenities," said Hamden McPete, coming from behind them and stepping suavely to the whiskey bottle and the smeary glass. He felt the need for a little pick-me-up.

"C'mon," said Josh, the more jittery and proactive of the two. "No need to hang around here. We have things to do and people to see." Turning toward McPete, he gave a little acknowledging nod. "Nice meeting you, sir."

"May good fortune attend your endeavors," McPete replied formally in his rolling baritone. He refilled and raised his glass. "May your luck be better than this whiskey." Which really wasn't saying much.

THIS IS NOBODY'S corporate headquarters," remarked Muldoon, looking at the remains of the cheap plywood door. "And it isn't where I'd expect a millionaire writer to be staying, either."

"'*Eccentric* millionaire.' You never heard that phrase?" asked Drake sarcastically, stepping through the shattered door. A tall, thin figure loomed up behind them, gold tooth flashing in an ingratiating smile.

"Gentlemen, I assume we all lookin' for the same thing, the great Halycon Sage," said Ratbone. "This is my associate, Mr. Wolf."

Wolf shifted nervously. He'd had a bit to do with cops in his time, and while Ratbone appeared to be trying to brazen it out, he would just as soon have run like hell. The four new arrivals looked around the room in vain. Though it had apparently been taken apart and searched by experts, there was no one in the room. No one there at all.

CHAPTER
FOURTEEN

ALYCON SAGE HAD finally found time out of his busy schedule to write another minimalist novel. In a sandy hollow beside a little, sparkling stream he lay back in satisfaction. By tomorrow morning he would have to take up the burden of his many insoluble problems and stagger on again, but for now he could relax, conscious of a job well done. The novel, as yet untitled, read:

> There was a man reading a book and it said there was a man reading a book and it said there was a man reading a book and it said there was a man reading a book and it said . . .

Like all his books, this one made a deeper point than was apparent on the surface. If no one does or creates anything original, if everyone merely reposts the sayings of others and lives vicariously through secondhand experience, eventually the only thing to read about or view will be someone reading about or viewing something. Whether anyone would get this subtle point was another matter.

And he had no idea how to punctuate a quote within a quote within a quote, since single and double quotes were the limits of his repertoire, but that also was another question for another day.

BASEL VASSELSCHNAUZER'S ASTOUNDING bull's eyes on the noses of the international agents had not come about by chance. When individuals are excessively annoying and unpleasant, their fellows tend to grudge them any credit, any recognition of the talents and good points they actually do possess. But nobody who had seen them, nobody in the snobbish private school or later in various pubs throughout England, Ireland, and Wales, had ever doubted the unparalleled, the amazing and reliable bull's eye-scoring talents of Deadeye Vasselschnauzer. In the split second when the door burst open, he had taken aim with both darts at once—and scored splendidly.

Later, for some reason, he had wakened before the two agents. He had looked around, seen a connecting door and opened it. Scuttling into the parking lot, he moved faster than he had in decades. A shiny black limousine awaited, and it called to all his instincts like the voice of a long-lost mother. "*I'm a limousine, Basel*," it whispered softly. "*I'm where you belong.*"

The beleaguered critic hastily dived into the back seat and concealed himself on the floor. The small gods of locks must have been with him that day because, like the connecting door in the motel room, this shiny door should have been barred to him, but wasn't. Thank Alexander Woollcott,[1] it wasn't.

 OSH AND TREVOR had gone away quite satisfied. It had been a strange morning, but they were pleased not to have been shot, and almost more pleased that the phantom corn fiber corporation would pose no threat to their scheme for dominating the virtual world through the best online computer game ever.

 OLF AND RATBONE had gotten away from Drake and Muldoon faster and more easily than Wolf would have believed possible. He was prepared for a major hassling session at best, or even a few nights in jail. As it was, the two obvious plainclothesmen simply rushed away. Though Wolf didn't know it, Muldoon had thought of another lead to investigate, while Drake was focused on clocking out and feeding his sugar addiction.

"What were you *thinking*, renting that limousine?" Wolf asked Ratbone. "The rest of the Dogs are gonna hang me out to *dry*! That was the last of our *money*!"

"Ours too, Wolfpup, ours too. I done borrowed as much as you did and more. But I got a kind of instinct at times, and today it was talkin' strong. *Get a limo*, it said. *Get a limo and the rest will follow*. Got to have faith, my man, got to have faith." Ratbone was probably the last African American in the universe who still called anybody "my man," but, as mentioned before, the Dogs and the Mofos existed in a time warp. They clung to their ancient slang.

---

1. Alexander Woollcott, an enormously influential New York theater critic and radio personality of the 20's and 30's, was known for his wit, his caustic tongue, and a somewhat obnoxious personality.

As they moved toward the car, something strange happened. They were approached by a small woman stepping out of a shadowed alley. She was dressed in a long, green-and-yellow-patterned skirt, a red-fringed shawl, and a bright green, red, and blue scarf that covered her head. She was all flying strands and swirling colors. Though she was not young, her hair was long and loose and her jewelry glinted in the sun. She looked like a Gypsy, which, in fact, she was—or more properly, a member of the Traveling People, a Romany woman.

"Mr. Rathbone," said the lady, looking him full in the face with her huge brown eyes, "There's another place for you. But you'll have to go and claim it. It won't come to you."

Ratbone was taken aback. She had called him *Rathbone*—his real name, which he hadn't heard in years—rather than *Ratbone*, as he was currently known to all. Then he shrugged it off, smiled at her politely, and gave her a coin for her trouble. "Chick's wack," he commented as they strolled off down the street, though he waited till she was out of earshot. "Crazy," he added to Wolf, whose slang was more out of date than his own by decades.

Ratbone put no credence in the woman's prediction. But indeed, far in the future, when Wolf was politely greeted at a church door by Deacon Augustus Rathbone, he would reflect that the guy hadn't really changed all that much. In spite of the perfect shave and the natural looking tooth that now replaced his gold one, Ratbone himself was the same. For he had always been inclined to help his fellow man.

"MAITREYA BUDDHA, AS a successor to Shakyamuni Buddha, will come when the Dharma is all but lost, unrecognizably altered, or ignored," read Sophie, mumbling to herself. "Well, we've got *that* one alright. Long earlobes:

don't know, never seen him. Unibrow: don't know, never seen him. Head bump: Don't know, never felt his head. Monk's robes. Oh, phooey, there aren't any pictures of him, how am *I* supposed to know!"

Sophie got up and made herself a sandwich, almost ready to give up her quest to prove that Halycon Sage was the Maitreya Buddha, the Buddha to Come. She couldn't find any proof. Maybe it was time to just finish her senior class graduation essay on *One Hundred and One Cows* without it.

LAYLA AND BROTHER Bob Hoskins, who did not know each other or Sophie, were having equally bad luck in their searches for the ultimate helpers or destroyers of mankind. Perhaps these three people were all psychically attuned somehow, because at the exact same moment as Sophie, the devout Muslim woman and the slightly mad evangelist also sighed, revised their plans, and went off to get a snack.

CHAPTER
FIFTEEN

REISCZECH WAS DRIVING himself crazy. Because all the messages but Ratbone's were obscene, he had convinced himself that Ratbone's message was the real article, a coded communication from the great Halycon Sage. He understood now the magnitude of the man he was dealing with, that his simple friend was world famous and hailed by almost everyone as a genius. Among the things the two shared was a delicacy approaching prudery. He felt certain that Sage could not have written any of the other messages.

Yet he could not bring himself to imagine that Sage had not responded at all, that he either *would* not or *could* not be found to come to the aid of Preisczech. The thought was too horrible to bear, and Preisczech was out of ideas. If this internet thing didn't work, he had nowhere else to turn. His scientific training, which might have told him that

Sage would not respond, was overridden by the greatness of his need. So, he just kept dialing the number, dialing the number.

The answers he got, all recordings, were supremely silly, often mentioning somebody called "Jenny." Assuming after the first few calls that the sender had entered one of the numbers incorrectly, he began methodically replacing each digit of the area code with a different number. The number of possible combinations, even of the first three digits, was daunting. Quickly he calculated it: 800, since no area codes started with one or zero.

After the first hour he had dialed many, many numbers. But through the same sort of madness that had dogged him in supermarkets across the country, every answer was a variation on one theme. "Jenny's not here," they said. And "Hi, I'm Jenny and I want to be with *you*," and "JENNY DOESN'T LIVE HERE, DAMMIT!" Preisczech began to wonder if he was really, truly going mad at last.

"Who in God's name is this Jenny?" he cried, once again from the depths of his soul, "Who is this Jenny, and why is she following me?"

WOLF KEPT THINKING he heard noises from the back of the limo. "What's that?" he asked Ratbone nervously.

"That's your brain sayin', let me out! Cause there's no room in this tiny, tiny head," said Ratbone, who was becoming irritable with the long drive and the twitchiness of his new friend. He had made a temporary alliance with this fool from the rival gang, touched in his essential kindness by the guy's sorry puppy eyes and his desperation to find Ruby. But now Ratbone was getting annoyed. He was used to putting up with the eccentricities of his own gang, but this rather small and miserable specimen of a Dirt Dog was something different altogether.

"I'm thirsty," said Wolf, who was starting to whine with tiredness.

"Get yourself a beer," said Ratbone. "And get me one, too. I put some in the back." His discretionary ghetto accent was falling off him. He was too exhausted to bother with it. Wolf was reaching around in back with his rather short arms. He came across a single bottle, held it up for inspection, held it upside down, then shook it. Nothing. Maybe a few drops, but that was all. He repeated this process a few more times, in the manner of a good scientist testing his hypothesis.

"Man, there ain't no beer back there, you *drank* it all."

"I didn't *drink* no beer. If it's gone, *you* musta drunk it," said Ratbone, slipping back into character to deal with the developing situation. If Wolf was going to drink all the beer and then pretend Ratbone had done it, their agreement was clearly off. It was back to business as usual. Ratbone wondered where he had put his brass knuckles and how Wolf had managed to drink all the beer without him noticing.

Wolf, meanwhile, was feeling around the back of the car, trying to ascertain whether or not any bottles remained. His hand came solidly down on something that felt very much like a knee. A knee in an elegant suit, dry-clean-only material such as his father had sometimes worn. Yes, it *was* a knee.

Wolf screamed. There was not supposed to be a knee in the back of the car. When Wolf screamed, Basel Vasselschnauzer screamed too. Wolf, in a panic, leaped out of the moving car. And Ratbone, too collected and seasoned to scream, merely drove off the road into a fancy, trash-compacting garbage truck.

There was silence. The garbage truck was parked; no driver was in sight. Either nobody had heard the accident, or nobody wanted to come out and deal with the crazy-looking characters around the limo.

"Whatchoo *doin'* back there?" cried Wolf when he could get his breath.

"Starting a circus. See, I brought my elephant," replied Vasselschnauzer caustically.

"You drank all *the beer*!"

Ratbone had gotten out and was inspecting the damage. He made soft little moaning noises. The shiny rented limousine would never be the same.

"Who *are* you?" persisted Wolf. The answer was predictable.

"*I'M* Basel *Vasselschnauzer.*"

"You mean that pissant little critic writes for the *Times*?" asked Ratbone, coming around to the window. "The one who cuts everybody off at the *knees*? The one with no *taste*?" Apparently there was more than one secret reader among the local gangs.

Vasselschnauzer began spluttering with rage. The splutter turned into an explosive, hacking cough.

"Geez, don't *die* on us," said Wolf, who never liked to see anyone too uncomfortable. The knife he carried was a total joke. He couldn't cut a salami.

"If you would provide me with some cough medicine, my good fellow, and a small glass of milk, some vodka with crushed ice, and a half a dozen oysters," said the critic, having recovered from his coughing fit. His manner of speaking assumed compliance.

Turning to Ratbone, he added, "I'm a bit short of a tip for you at the moment, my man, but that can be adjusted later." He waved his hand gracefully, indicating largesse. For once Ratbone was speechless. He had been mistaken for a limo driver. Perhaps Wolf had been cast in the critic's mind as an eccentric millionaire.

Wolf started laughing. Ratbone shook his head in disbelief and folded his long frame back into the car.

"And a new suit is obviously necessary," continued Vasselschnauzer, oblivious to the reactions he was getting. "The address of my tailor—"

Calmly, Ratbone engaged the partition separating passenger and driver, but he could still see Vasselschnauzer waving and jumping around in the rearview mirror. It was disturbing. For that matter, he could still hear him.

"Oysters, dammit, **HALF A DOZEN OYSTERS!**" shrieked Basel Vasselschnauzer. His urbanity was all surface, a thin, thin earth's-crust over the red-hot lava of his petulance.

"And **VODKA WITH CRUSHED ICE! I NEED IT! IT'S *MEDICINAL!***"

Wolf was not a lot of help. He had fallen over laughing, possibly laid low by the stresses of the day. It was certainly not turning out as planned.

"**OYSTERS!**" shrieked Basel Vasselschnauzer. "**CHAMPAIGNE! CRUSHED ICE! VODKA! *MUSHROOMS!!!***"

"***COUGH SYRUP,***" he added when he could get his breath again.

"We got to tie him up," muttered Rathbone as he pulled away from the curb. "I bees a humane man, but we got to tie him *up*. And *gag* him."

Rathbone's intuition was still cranking in high gear, and something told him to hang on to this insufferable pipsqueak rather than just kicking him out of the car. But for the moment he was too tired to buy a rope, so he just kept driving.

CHAPTER
SIXTEEN

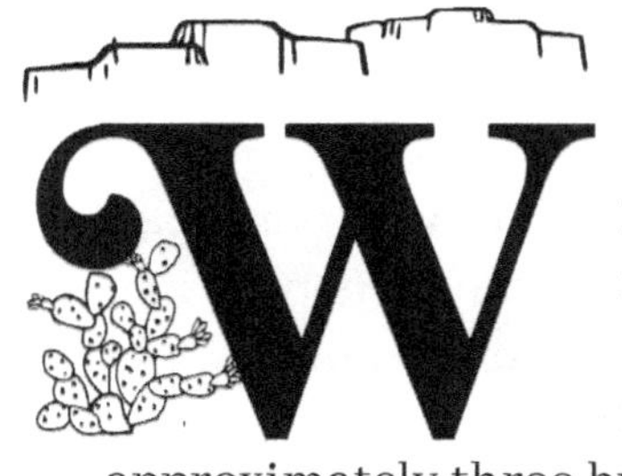

ITHOUT THE STEADYING influence of the kindly Halycon Sage, Preisczech was becoming more and more confused. After approximately three hundred phone calls, none of which connected him with a living person, he began to develop an *idée fixe,* an obsessive idea that lodged in his mind. Had he thought to search the phone number on the internet, he might have saved himself a lot of trouble. But somehow the thought never occurred to him.

If he could not find Halycon Sage—and it began to look as if he couldn't—perhaps he needed to find this *Jenny* Logically one could not dial three hundred essentially random numbers without ever reaching a human being, but that was just what was happening. They were all recordings, voice mails, machines. And none of them ever said, "I'll get back to you. How unlikely was that? By the ordinary laws of probability, practically impossible.

Preisczech did not have Halycon Sage's horror of machines and bureaucracy. He had grown up in the shadow of a post-Soviet police state. To him, the fact that Jenny was so well guarded meant she was *important.* Perhaps if he could find her, she would help him. Certainly *somebody* needed to help him. The weight of the cigar box and the whistle—what was in them and what they signified—had become too great. The cigar box was too heavy for his heart to carry. His heart, so long denied in the shadow of his mad but brilliant brain.

Putting the phone down, he stretched his aching back and arms and stepped into the hall, taking in the cabbage and curry smells of his rooming house. It was 1:00 a.m. and the silence was palpable. He went back to bed. Nothing had changed out there or in his room, but something had changed in Preisczech. Perhaps the frozen fish in his soul had begun to thaw. Perhaps he could find Jenny. And perhaps she would be kind.

"Where *are* you, Jenny?" he called into the darkened rooming house. "Shaddup, ya moron!" came the dependable reply from one of his fellow roomers. Turning on his side and favoring his telephone arm, Preisczech sighed and went to sleep.

S OMEONE ELSE BESIDES Preisczech had begun to thaw, had begun to experience a fundamental change within. The much-tested Muhammad Abdurraheem Hussein had reached the end of his rope. He had accepted the challenges of the West, of modernity and materialism. He had believed that if he put all the old things behind him—the warrens of red and sand-colored houses, the desert stars, beautiful enough to break your heart, but leading nowhere—that he could succeed. He had channeled everything into his studies, his career. And *now* look at him—he had nothing. And he had not been a failure, that was the horror of it. He had been a great success. But because of his name, appearance, and heredity, none of this had mattered.

He had been a co-worker and neighbor to many (though too busy to make friends), but where were they now? In all the surrounding McMansions with their obsessively green lawns, had there been one human being to step forward on his behalf? To say, "This is a good man, a good citizen. He mows his lawn, pays his taxes, works hard. He bothers nobody." There had been no one. Like others before him, Abdurraheem was discovering the cold, poisoned heart of materialism, the shallow emptiness of its promise for which the poor, the desperate, and the wrongly guided give their families and their souls. He realized all of this, and all he could do was weep.

When Layla returned from her fruitless library searches, leading little Nuri by the hand, he was still sitting on the same curb, leaning on the cat carrier in a puddle of tears. Layla had no idea how to deal with her husband, who had gone from driven careerist to heart-broken failure with no intervening stages other than his increasing desperation. They couldn't go on sitting there forever. Little Nuri was patient, but the child was only five. And the poor cat was meowing pitifully.

"Dude, it can't be *that* bad," came a voice. *Not a Voice, but a human voice anyway, that was something*, thought Layla. So, what was this stranger?

Looking up, she saw a smallish, scruffy man, bearded and longhaired. His eyes and furrowed brow looked concerned— for herself, apparently, and for her husband and the child. Behind him, like a friendly jinn, stood a tall, thin Black man. He smiled, flashing a gold tooth. Nuri seemed enchanted with him, ignoring the small man, and staring at the golden smile. Abdurraheem sat unresponsive.

"Dude, have you *eaten?*"asked the small man. Abdurraheem thought about it. No, they had not. Nuri must be starving.

"What do you suggest?" he responded in a tired voice. These were some sort of street people or hippies or people on welfare. Once he would have scorned them, had no time for them. But now they were all he had; his proud neighbors had ignored him in his time of need. *Like that Good Samaritan thing the Christians have*, he thought.

"We going to the Dirty Dog," said the Black man decisively, giving Nuri a hand up off the curb. "I know it sound bad to you, but it be a *warm* place."

PREISCZECH HAD TAKEN to stopping random strangers on the street and asking them where Jenny was. If they asked, "Jenny who?" he just looked blank. Though his fundamental being had experienced a seismic shift, he was outwardly desperate and approaching the near-catatonic state in which Halycon Sage had first found him.

One of his aunts had told him of the great rabbis of Eastern Europe, the Hasidim, who taught that asking a stranger could sometimes provide information, holy guidance. Or perhaps they didn't, maybe he had heard this somewhere else. But he was beyond reason now, and almost beyond hope, so any course would do.

Down the street came a small woman, all shawls and colors, fringes and blowing hair. "Have you seen Jenny?" he asked her.

Huge, mournful brown eyes looked into his, studying him carefully. "You believe you have no friends except the One Who Can't Be Found. But this is not true. Though they do not understand you, those others are your friends. They mean you well."

Preisczech knew exactly what she was talking about. Returning home, he showered, shaved, put on his best clothes and headed for the Dirty Dog.

THE IRAQI FAMILY found it a little odd that the two hippies were driving a limousine. The tall Black man had introduced himself as "Ratbone," for which both adults blamed their faulty English. This could not possibly be anyone's name.

They could make nothing of the ranting little man in the back seat, who kept demanding oysters and caviar. Like the other grown-ups in the car, they ignored him. But Nuri, seated quietly in back like the good child he was, began repeating softly, after a while, "*I'M-Basel*-Vasselschnauzer. *I'M*-Basel-Vasselschnauzer." It was the best English word he had ever heard.

When they got to the Dirty Dog, a surprise was waiting: Preisczech was back, all dressed up like Christmas. But nothing could be done about him now — there was a family to feed and care for.

"Hey Bill," called Wolf to the bartender. "Haul out some of those pickled eggs, willya? And some peanuts. What else you got?"

"I got some pork rinds," offered Bill helpfully.

"That ain't right," said Ratbone. "You don't want no pork rinds, do you?"

Abdurraheem shuddered. He was sitting in the Dirty Dog and he was being offered pork rinds. It figured.

"They don't eat no pork," said Ratbone to the bartender.

"Got it," said Bill. "How about a ham sandwich?"

"They don't eat that neither," said Ratbone, "but the cat might like some. Got any buffalo wings?"

Abdurraheem was pretty sure that buffaloes were like cows. They did not have wings. But at least it wasn't pig meat. He nodded an okay.

Layla, deep in a *dua* prayer of thankfulness, saw the symbolism differently from her depressed husband. Like blessed Yusuf, Maryam, and baby Isa, peace be upon them, her beleaguered family had found shelter in a stable. Well, in a bar actually, but this was no time to be picky. Little Nuri would sleep warm, with a full stomach.

It turned out that the back room had a couple of cots in it, and the exhausted family was led there after they had eaten.

"What about *me?*" grumbled Buzzard.

"Where am *I* going to sleep?" whined Snake Eyes. He was seconded by various other members of the Dirty Dog Gang.

"On the floor. Or the bar," said Bill unsympathetically. "Or go home to ya *muddas.*" This made the Dog Boys sad. It was possible that, like Peter Pan's accomplices, they *had* no mothers.

CHILDREN MAKE ODD combinations of the words they hear from others. Nuri drifted off to sleep mumbling: "*Alhamdulillah. I'mbaselVasselschnauzer. Alhamdulillah. I'mbaselVasselschnauzer.*" To him these long and fragrant phrases seemed not unalike.

AFTER THE LITTLE family was put to bed, there were several other matters to be ironed out. One was the presence of Ratbone, de facto head of the Fifth Street Mofos, which was unusual. Not unprecedented, but unusual. There had been "gang summits" and other negotiations in the Dirty Dog before. Despite its unappealing name, it had a certain ambiance. And, though both groups studiously ignored the fact, their infrequent gatherings were becoming less like meetings between mortal enemies, and more like family reunions. Still, for Ratbone to be here alone, for all the world like another, taller Dirty Dog, was unusual, and broke with precedent.

"It's okay, he's with me," said Wolf, to some skeptical grumbling. "He's our computer expert," he tried next. "C'mon, guys, he's helping me find Ruby."

"And this fool Halycon Sage, too," chimed in Ratbone.

The group unbent a little. If it was for Ruby . . .

The next thing on the agenda was the reappearance of Preisczech, who seemed a bit crestfallen at his distracted reception.

"Hey, sorry to ignore you, dude," said Buzzard in a friendly way. "We've had a lot on our minds these last couple-a hours. Whatchoo been doin', man?"

Skull and Snake Eyes gathered round, clapping his back in a friendly way. Beaner was over by the bar, also watching, but Ruby was nowhere to be seen.

Preisczech began to feel better. "I've invented something," he said, holding up the cigar box. "Something new."

He had their full attention. Suddenly he wondered how much he should tell them, but with so many eyes on him, it seemed wrong to clam up now. "And I have another new name," he added, hoping to distract them.

He did, in fact, have a new name. He had invented it after watching a lot of 40's movies and reading a bunch of early noire novels. The name was composed of two words by which the male characters addressed each other constantly. In almost three weeks, it had only gotten him a few odd looks. And no laughter, which was always a plus. He stuck out his hand, determined to play out his introduction scene correctly at last.

"The name's Mac," he said. "Buddy Mac." Buddy Mac was not too bad, considering. The Dirty Dogs, one by one, shook his hand. They really did feel a sneaking affection for Preisczech, and they felt a little guilty for letting him hang around unacknowledged while they got the family settled. "Better than Flintstone Exlax like before," said Skull. "You're learning. You'll be a real American one of these days."

"So, whatcha got in the box, Mac? Since you're one of us now," asked Beaner, walking over with his drink. He ignored the annoying "real American" comment, reflecting that these ignorant *norte Americanos* had no idea that Canadians, Mexicans, and people a long way south *of that* were real Americans too. On acounta the whole deal was called *the Americas.* But after fifteen years, he had given up trying to make this point.

"Whatcha got in the box?" he repeated.

"Nanobots," Preisczech blurted.

There was silence. Nobody had any idea what he was talking about. Ruby said things like this at times, probably trying to prove how intelligent she was, and it was best to just ignore it. The college-educated should never be encouraged in their snobbery.

"Nanobots," said Preisczech more loudly, wondering if somehow they had not heard him.

"I knew a *Nan Abbott* once," said Snake Eyes thoughtfully. "She pronounced it different, though." The conversation was at an impasse.

Preisczech thought a bit more information might break through the inexplicable wall of incomprehension now separating him from his friends.

"Robots. You can't see them. They're invisible, because very small, you see. Very, very small. That what means *nano.*" His English was deserting him again, slipping away as it always did when he was under stress. To be almost accepted, then to fall back again into strangerhood, this would be unbearable.

"And *bots* for *robots.* Little, tiny robots, too small to see. Red and silver," he added proudly. "I get color idea from kid game I find online. Red and silver."

Like Josh and Trevor after conceiving their own Lazlex site, he had checked to make sure he was the first. Though he wasn't, he had seen no conflict. Still, he had been intrigued enough to look around and had been charmed by the red and silver of the tiny robots in the Lazlex game. It had inspired him to hastily alter the molecular makeup of his nanobots to replicate those colors. This took him barely half an hour. Such was his genius.

He had also appropriated the idea of starting with nuclear plants and weapons. The nanobots would begin by dismantling the most deadly inventions, working their way down to relatively harmless things like cars and computers. If at some point he wanted to stop them, he had only to blow his silent whistle. The whistle was always round his neck and the nanobots were safe in their unassailable box of strange new metal, so all was well.

Coming out of his momentary reverie, Preisczech found everyone staring at him. "But all okay, though, nothing to worry about," he persisted, wondering if it was the awe and wonder of the nanobots that held them speechless. "See, I have *whistle*." He lifted the whistle from around his neck, showing them all was well.

"So, no problem, no danger. I want them, I call them. With whistle, they obey me. So, is no problem."

Still nothing. He was beginning to feel a little desperate.

"And they make more of them," he added obscurely, trying one last time. "Metal, plastic, leaves, paper: is *matter*, they can make more. Any material. Forever, never stop."

The pained silence continued. Giving up explaining as a bad job, he did something he believed would always work, in any country. "Drinks?" he asked.

And everyone forgot the nanobots.

CHAPTER
SEVENTEEN

**ULDOON, HAVING COME** up empty on Lazlex, was back at his computer, simply seeking anomalous behavior, looking for odd things. And the three hundred telephone calls that one man had made to 867-5309 were very odd indeed. Sure, once in a while somebody called this number for a laugh or out of curiosity, and most of those who had been saddled with it had had it changed. But three hundred calls?

Muldoon pulled up the source of the calls and in seconds connected with an email address. He found paydirt right away. His target was the person who had established the new Lazlex website, the one about corn fibers. His instincts were correct; there was something here. Searching the history and emails, he quickly found a visit to the *other*

Lazlex site, the really interesting one with the red and silver robots. Tiny, tiny robots, running all around to the actual locations of secret nuclear sites and doing something that froze Muldoon's blood.

He pulled up an address and viewed the building that housed his target, apparently a rundown rooming house. For once, risking his career and the possibility of criminal prosecution, he did not wait for official permission to wipe his nose. He was "in the zone," and he requisitioned the amazing surveillance machine and the black van with such authority and such fire in his eye that refusal was unthinkable.

An hour later he was on his way, unmarked black van crammed with expensive technology. Not just the usual stuff, but the budget-busting machine that heard and saw through walls, and microscopically at that. In light of emerging circumstances, this apparently ridiculous invention might be just what the doctor ordered.

HALYCON SAGE DID not *want* to write *Boo Radley Goes Hawaiian*. After his initial enthusiasm, the idea bored him. And he realized that, given the complexity of the material, it would have to be about five times as long as anything he had previously written. This thought plunged him into an agony of writer's block.

He did not want to go into town either, after writing the detestable book, to find an internet café, check his emails, and send in his draft. Kathryn, his editor, would be hopping up and down, scolding him electronically for his lack of diligence and demanding to know his whereabouts. Though generally a reasonable person, she became unreasonable on the subject of deadlines.

Halycon Sage, sitting beside a shining stream, shaded by purple mountains and warmed by a perfect milk-pour of yellow sun, picked up his pen and wrote:

Boo Radley sat . . .
Boo Radley stood . . .
Boo Radley waited . . .

Breathing in sagebrush, eucalyptus, and the special smell of wet willow trees along the water, the special, beloved smell of the West, he wrote:

Nobody had expected Boo Radley to . . . and
"Hawaii!" thought Boo Radley.

It was no good. He hated the thing. He wanted to get back to his *real* work, the novel that was currently struggling to be born out of his sensitive artist's unconscious: *The Land Before Time Forgot Itself.*

MULDOON PEERED THROUGH the solid wall from his vantage point across the street. No one was there, and there was nothing of much interest in the room. No gun, apparently. No explosives, not even a Superman-type change of wardrobe in the closet or the drawers. The clothes inside, which Muldoon could see with ease, were dull and brown and gray-green, the clothes of a man with no interest in such things. He scanned his way across the room. There was nothing in the tiny kitchenette area, nothing out of the ordinary anywhere. Nothing in the bathroom . . .

Muldoon stopped moving. Low down on the far bathroom wall was an odd little storage cupboard, one of those things you find in old houses. In it was what appeared to be a cigar box. Funny place to keep a cigar box . . . He zoomed in closer. To his sensitive instruments the box appeared to be made of metal, but metal painted to look like cheap wood, which was *also* odd. It was rare to see cigar boxes anymore, those ubiquitous carryalls for everything in Muldoon's childhood.

They were what you kept your treasures in. Every kid had them. You still saw them once in a while, but not made of metal, much less metal painted to imitate wood. He focused on the box and fiddled with the controls. Micro level.

Muldoon held his breath. He could not see inside the box. He could see through doors and walls, through wood and stucco and cement. He could see through steel, but he could not see through that cigar box. So, this was no ordinary metal, no ordinary material at all. He adjusted the machine to its finest microscopic focus . . . more, more . . . steady . . . He could see through the box. The things he saw inside seemed to be swarming, moving all around in purposeful activity. Tiny things, even under extreme magnification. Red and silver.

Muldoon left the car, creeping closer. He did something to the outer door and entered. He did the same thing to the room door. He walked into the bathroom, picked up the strange cigar box. Yes, it was much heavier than it should have been. He made no attempt to open it. If he was right about what it contained, that would be the worst thing *anyone* could do, short of launching a nuclear bomb. Anyway, it was someone else's problem; all he had to do was bring it in. The agent shifted the box, concealing it beneath his coat, and walked out the door. His triumph was short-lived.

"Freeze!" shouted two voices, one British, one American. *Oh, come on*, thought Muldoon. *Does anybody say freeze anymore?* But he followed instructions. Of course there had to be somebody bigger than him in on this. Somebody had to be onto Preisczech. And not just his superiors at the nameless national agency. *International* agents, presumably, getting under the feet of honest working cops. Ready to steal the glory and blow the cover. As usual. His face betrayed nothing. He stood there.

"Would you mind giving me that?" inquired the blonde-haired woman with the British voice. "We have to open it."

Muldoon handed it over. She was pointing a gun at him. "I wouldn't do that if I were you, though," said Muldoon.

"Why not?"

Because it's full of invisible, killer robots that are going to take apart the planet, he wanted to say. *And if you let them out, no one will ever get them back.* But since he had no idea whom they represented, he kept his mouth shut.

"He doesn't know anything," said the woman dismissively. "Let's go." And they did. The man with her had spoken not a word.

CHAPTER
EIGHTEEN

AVE YOU SEEN Jenny?" Preisczech asked Wolf, sitting at the bar in the Dirty Dog. He didn't really expect him to know, but just on the off chance …

He hadn't checked on the cigar box lately. The Jenny obsession was driving other matters out of his awareness.

"Huh?" inquired Wolf, who had a hangover.

"Do you know how I can get hold of Jenny?" persisted Preisczech.

"Sure, man, just call 867-5309," said Wolf and laughed uproariously.

"You *know* her?" blurted Preisczech, amazement and hope lighting his face like a sunrise.

"No, man, no, it's a *song*," gasped Wolf, taking pity.

"A song?" asked Preisczech blankly.

"Yeah. I GOT it, I GOT it, I got your NUMber on the wall," Wolf sang tunelessly. "I GOT it, for a GOOD TIME CALL. Somebody wrote her number on the wall. In the song. Sounds kind of gross, but it's a great song."

This can't be happening, thought Preisczech in his native language. *Is my life really just a joke, then? Is it really?* Suddenly he saw her in his mind so clearly, his Jenny. Soft curling hair, light brown; soft brown eyes and a pretty mouth; a sweet, gentle voice and gentle hands. She had to be real. She had to.

He passed it off with a laugh, suave and casual as always. He and Wolf talked of other matters. But it was hard to wait, hard to wait until Wolf had gone away and everyone's attention was elsewhere. He didn't really think there would be information about her in the restroom of the Dirty Dog. But he could not stop himself from looking, just in case.

Ms. LYDIA WENTWORTH-BREWSTER and Mr. Sean Raintree looked in awe at the box, passing it back and forth, feeling its weight.

"Whoever made this was a *meticulous* craftsman," remarked Raintree.

Though it looked like an ordinary wooden cigar box, rather battered, its weight indicated a heavy metal. Not only that: though there was no apparent lock, there was no way to open it. The lid just stayed shut.

"Pry it," said Lydia.

"Tried that," said Sean.

"Drop it," said Lydia.

"Explosives," said Sean.

"Run it through the scanner," said Lydia.

"Got it," said Sean, and they headed back to where the equipment was. Apparently the box did not contain explosives.

"Drop something *on* it," said Lydia.

They tried to crush the box, but it wouldn't crush.

"Shoot the lock," said Lydia.

There *was* no lock.

"Blow torch," said Lydia.

They tried, concentrating on the top of the box where the lid appeared to touch the body, the part that would have opened had the box been normal. It got a little warm, but otherwise, nothing.

"Blow it up, dammit," said Lydia.

And they did, using a remarkably powerful material, capable of targeting a very small area. A sort of desktop equivalent of a smart bomb. They covered the same area they'd gone over with the blowtorch. The box did not explode, but it did open. Even Preisczech's genius was not absolutely fail-safe.

There was nothing in the box. They stared.

"It's empty," said Lydia.

And now, it was.

CHAPTER
NINETEEN

ABDURRAHEEM SAT SILENT, tears falling. "I don't know what to do with him," said Layla. The Dirty Dog Boys and Bill the bartender had tried this and that to cheer him up, but nothing worked.

Abdurraheem sat silent, tears falling. He had tried his best, —but nothing had worked out. He was out of energy, courage, hope, and ideas. He was such a mess, you'd have thought he'd been reading a Niemand Kompt novel. But it was more like Halycon Sage, really.

"And a man went forth, and he did everything right. But everything went wrong anyway. The End," thought Abdurraheem, who had memorized Halycon Sage's third and greatest novel. *That's the story of my life. The story of my life.* Though he did not drink, he was in a bar, and perhaps something of its ambience was affecting him. He was passing from real despair into maudlin repetition. He had nothing. Nothing.

"C'mon, you can stay with me," said Buzzard with a sigh, finally, after all these years, giving up and blowing his cover. For Buzzard was very wealthy, and he had a big house with many rooms when he bothered to go back to it. And he *did* have a mother, an anxious, doting one.

Silence.

"What about some home cooking?" persisted Buzzard. "Arabian style? Lebanese? Marcel can cook anything, any cuisine."

Silence.

"And I know a lawyer, man, he's *magic*. He can find you a job, a good one."

Abdurraheem lifted his head a little in response to this.

"Interesting work with good pay and benefits," Buzzard went on. "Probably not flying, though," he finished a little doubtfully.

As in a dream, Buzzard's speech had altered, revealing him as someone else.

"*Buzzard*," said Abdurraheem. He was incredulous.

"*Anthony*," said the other with a shame-faced grin.

Abdurraheem stared at him. "But if you have all that, why do you . . . ?"

Silence.

After a moment, Buzzard looked up, his blue eyes clear.

"'*Less*. I wanted *less* out of life,'" he quoted. Good old Agatha Christie.[1] Sometimes she hit the nail right on the head.

PREISCZECH FIGURED THE contest between himself and life was currently at a draw. He had friends now, and a place to be. They were incapable of understanding

---

1. From *The Burden,* one of six psychological novels Agatha Christie published as Mary Westmacott. Usually appearing with trashy-looking romance covers and absurdly inaccurate descriptive blurbs, some of these books are little masterpieces of insight and character.

the nanobots, or anything else about him really, but they were not laughing at him either. He had been accepted.

The sadness in his newly wakened heart, which would turn to agony if he let it, he steadfastly refused to deal with. He would simply shut it out and drink more vodka. Surprisingly, the Dirty Dog had very good vodka. He sat silent on his barstool, for the moment neither happy nor sad. Numb.

"Are you cold?" asked a soft voice. "You look cold."

Preisczech turned and looked. A girl sat beside him. Her eyes were gentle, an odd chocolate brown, softly glowing. Everything about her looked soft, and Preisczech wanted to touch her white skin. Her light brown hair hung in feathery curls. She had a bit too much make-up on, but it didn't matter. She looked shy, and he didn't want to frighten her.

"Jenny?" he asked, hardly daring to hope.

"Sure, I'm Jenny," said the girl, her eyes a little wild. She was trembling.

"What's *your* name?"

"Preisczech," said Preisczech, forgetting his many aliases.

They sat at a loss, not knowing what to do with each other, but closer than might have been expected.

"Is that your *first* name?" asked the girl, a little flummoxed by the rolling syllables.

Her quiet voice filled his heart with delight. She was quite young, maybe twenty-two. She wore a soft cotton dress, with flowers on it.

"No, of course not," said Preisczech, suddenly comfortable in English. "It's Alexander. Alex," he amended. That was better, less imposing.

"Alex," said Jenny, trying it out. It pleased her somehow. It was a *nice* name.

Preisczech couldn't believe it. His Jenny was sitting beside him. He had found her.

They sat in silence for a while.

"Coffee?" asked Preisczech, indicating with his head that they would find it elsewhere.

"If you want," said Jenny shyly, taking his hand.

Preisczech, in his state of high inebriation and the wonder of this meeting, wanted to give her the earth. He had no earth to give, nor even the moon, so he drew the battered whistle from around his neck and carefully, ceremoniously, he placed it over her head. It was an odd thing to do, giving her a battered tin whistle as though it were the crown jewels.

They sat a little longer. Then, feeling safe at last, wanted at last, in the right place at long, long last, they strolled out together into the cool, sweet evening.

RATBONE HAD FINALLY found a rope. Now, bound and gagged in an alcove in the recently vacated back room, the exceedingly annoying Basel Vasselschnauzer spotted a novel by Niemand Kompt, kicked into a corner with some dust and dead flies. Who had brought *that* abomination here? At least it had ended up in the right place. If Basel had not been busy chasing the chimera of Halycon Sage, he would have noticed the meteoric rise of this monster and crushed him like a bug.

For it had turned out, amazingly enough, that Basel Vasselschnauzer really did have standards, revealed to himself for the first time by the repugnant writing of Niemand Kompt.

One did not need to know that the man was a self-professed nihilist, a detestable, bragging one. Hopelessness and discouragement seeped from every page, snideness and cynicism that sapped the reader, sucking out his confidence, while a certain undeniable talent kept him spellbound in the horrid author's sticky web.

The name "Niemand Kompt"—"Nobody's Coming"—had been chosen quite deliberately. It meant that Jesus was not coming, nor the Mahdi, nor the Maitreya Buddha nor the

Moschiach.[1] It meant that no one waited on the higher planes or in the inner depths to welcome home the tired traveler. That no inspiration would rise within oneself to make sense of it all, to light the way, to challenge the chaotic, banal madness that had eaten the world.

True love was not coming either. The electrician was not coming, nor the man to fix the steps. No friend was coming to inquire after one's health, or why one's Facebook page was so long silent.

No one would do anything about the tsunami victims or the nuclear meltdown. No one cared enough to try. They would go on reading about celebrities instead.

For Basel Vasselschnauzer, the hopelessness that seeped from Niemand Kompt had a particular meaning. He would never get home to his green silk and his black marble, tastefully veined with white. He would never get his mushrooms. He would never again sit outside a Paris café with his friends, feeling the gentle sunlight, demolishing some author. *"This was not the Paris where good Americans go when they die,"* thought Vasselschnauzer, quoting one of his heroes.[2] The quote was not quite accurate and not quite apt, but he was tired.

Suddenly, in an apotheosis brought on by the trials of the last twenty-four hours, Basel chose his side. What was the opposite of Niemand Kompt, apostle of pretentious despair and chilling, cheap meaninglessness, of emptiness disguised as art and style? What was the opposite of this? Because whatever it was, Basel Vasselschnauzer would fight to the death for it. The attack-badger side of him was real, and at this moment it assumed a new form.

---

1. "Messiah" in Hebrew. Not Jesus. The Jewish Messiah is expected to bring world peace (yes, even in the Middle East) and restore the Earth to the pristine state of Eden. Clearly that has not happened yet.

2. Elliot Templeton in Somerset Maugham's *The Razor's Edge.*

The answer came to him so simply, so cleanly.

The opposite of Niemand Kompt was *Halycon Sage*. Halycon Sage was life, simplicity, Reality, the breath of mystery—the thing we all believe before we don't. That was Halycon Sage.

And Basel Vasselschnauzer, who had never done anything worthwhile in all his fifty-seven years, managed to spit out his gag and began gnawing through his ropes.

MULDOON FELT LIKE a new man. Suddenly he had a better job title, a bigger budget, and the confidence of his superiors. Expecting to be blamed, demoted, or worse for the loss of the cigar box, which he had reported accurately at no small risk to himself, he was stunned to find himself commended, promoted and on a plane to Washington to meet with Higher Authority.

Finally he was getting a chance to use his excellent cop skills, his fine detectival instincts. For like many good trackers, he was developing a feeling for his prey. Not some Hemingway nonsense where fish and man become one (Fishman!), but an honest sense of his target and how he thought about things. It was really almost like a psychic sense, though he wouldn't be saying that around the office.

The man's name was Alexander Preisczech and he had come from Eastern Europe. He had used several absurd pseudonyms and he acted like someone on the run from the law, though for what crime Muldoon could not determine. Perhaps some government was after him. He was neurotic, a loner. Scientific background. Highly intelligent. Above all, obsessive, driven. Narrowly focused. A man of many quirks. Muldoon thought with satisfaction of the upcoming meeting and all he had to share.

Drake slept contentedly on the plane next to Muldoon, his head against the window. He was getting his plane trip at last. Though everything from the airport atmosphere to the airplane food (or lack of it) had changed for the worse since the last time he'd traveled, he was content. They still offered some pretty good whiskey.

RUBY, HAVING PUT certain things together with the undeniable though silent aid of Stupid, had returned to the Dirty Dog. She did not want to upset the Boys, whom she thought of as essentially slow and conservative, easily shocked, so she came in quietly through the back, wanting to see what was going on and pick her moment to reveal herself.

She never got the chance. Rather, she collided in the door with a small, mouse-haired man, his elegant clothes wreathed in dustballs. He seemed to be in a terrific hurry.

"Who the hell are you?" asked Ruby.

"*I'm* Basel *Vasselschnauzer*," he replied, drawing himself up.

"Well, don't whine about it, we all have our problems," said Ruby.

"*I'm* going to find *Halycon Sage*," declared Basel Vasselschnauzer.

"You and everybody else," said Ruby, "but *I* know where he is." She thought a moment. Maybe she could use an assistant, albeit a somewhat clueless-looking one. "Come on, Faffenhauser, let's blow this popstand."

As they were leaving, she stooped to pick up a long rope that lay, somewhat surprisingly, on the open floor near the doorway. It was unexpectedly strong.

"Here, you hold on to this," she told Vasselschnauzer. And, silent for once, he wound it up and tied it loosely round his waist.

Ruby *did know* where Halycon Sage was—she and Stupid *both* knew—but once again she was foiled by the presence of an unexpected intruder. From behind a corner of the building stepped a shadowy figure holding a gun, and the gun was pointed right at Basel Vasselschnauzer. Ruby could have taken it away from him—she was that fast—but Vasselschnauzer was an unknown quantity and she couldn't risk his life.

Very shortly, once Preisczech's nanobots really got going, the gun would be useless. But none of them knew this, and anyway, it did them no good now. Ruby, entirely out of character, bowed to the inevitable.

BUT WHERE WAS No-Name Stupid? Surely the brown and white pinto was not sitting abandoned in some nameless motel, or wandering the freeways of the Southwest. Was anyone *feeding* Stupid? Who was taking care of him? For he could not procure apples and instant oatmeal by *himself.* While he was certainly smart enough to accomplish this small feat, he had no money, no pockets, no opposable thumbs, and he didn't speak English.

SITTING BESIDE HIS little, shining stream, Halycon Sage wrote:

Boo Radley Goes Hawaiian

Boo Radley stood on his porch like a pale mushroom. He had made this enormous step—of standing on his porch in full daylight—since the night the little girl had taken his hand and changed his world.

But it really wasn't quite enough to compensate for an entire, wasted life, so Boo Radley bought a ticket to Hawaii. Once there, he got himself in shape and learned to swim. The tuquoise ocean sparkled and the sun glowed gold. White sea birds sailed above the habor. The air was filled with flowers.

Pounds of pale flab melted away and Boo became a nice, golden brown. (Not too muscular; just right.) He made many friends who were charmed by his listening skills. One day, while he was surfing, he met a beautiful young Hawaiian lady and they fell in love.

The End

NOTE: Because Halycon Sage wanted everything in the story to be perfect, he had taken 20 or 30 years off Boo's age as part of his makeover.

Halycon Sage put down his pen. This was the longest novel he had ever written, practically Tolstoy compared to his previous work. Somebody *else* could figure out where to break it into chapters for the serial rights. There was only one problem. To get it to his editor, he would have to head into town and use his email.

OF COURSE THE kidnapper was Niemand Kompt, finally driven over the edge of madness by Basel Vasselschnauzer's incendiary review. There is a certain inevitability about these things. He, too, had been tracking Halycon Sage, of whom he was insanely jealous, recognizing him as his nemesis. That Sage had never contacted him or written about him increased his fury. He wanted the hero to think well of him, to recognize his evil genius, and Sage's obliviousness filled him with rage.

His search had led to Preisczech. Kompt had been concealed in the shadows in a dark corner of the bar when Preisczech explained about the whistle. He understood what had escaped the clueless Dog Gang, and the slightly smarter Ratbone: This was ultimate power.

With the Whistle of Doom, he could control the nanobots. The microscopically invisible, eternally self-replicating nanobots. He could make them do his bidding. By any means necessary, he could become the greatest author in the world, known to everyone, spreading the poison gas of his perspective to every corner of the earth.

And no one would even remember Halycon Sage.

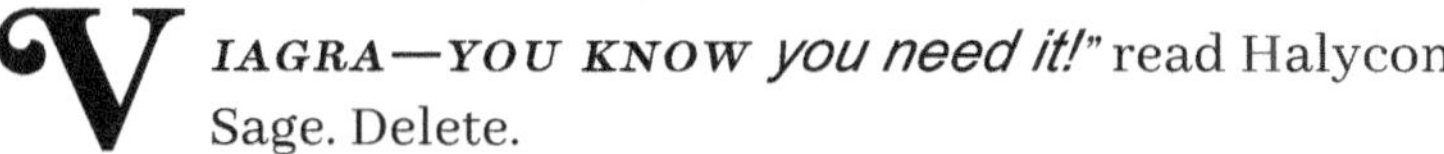

"VIAGRA—YOU KNOW *you need it!*" read Halycon Sage. Delete.

He had sent in his manuscript from the internet café, but he felt an obligation, a residual tug from his former life, to at least scan his messages. His eyes glazed over with boredom at the nonsense filling his inbox.

Delete.

Delete.

Delete.

What was this? Another Nigerian Letter?

Dear friend,

I have had to flee my country with a hundred million dollars that my wicked uncle tried to take from me. I only need some kind and sensitive person such as yourself to help me deposit it. Please send me your bank account number and password . . .

Delete . . . Wait a minute. What was this next one?

HALYCON SAGE,

YOU DON'T KNOW ME, BUT I KNOW YOU. I HAVE VASSELSCHNAUZER AND A GIRL CALLED RUBY. IF YOU DO NOT MEET ME ON TOP OF THE VLASCO BUILDING AT 11:31 P.M. TOMORROW (JUNE 28TH), VASSELSCHNAUZER WILL DIE.

OH, AND THE GIRL RUBY WILL DIE TOO.
BRING WITH YOU THE APPARENTLY
ORDINARY TIN WHISTLE THAT PREISCZECH
WEARS AROUND HIS NECK.
DO NOT TRY TO SUBSTITUTE ANOTHER
WHISTLE, OR I WILL KNOW. I WANT THAT ONE,
THE ONE THAT CONTROLS THE NANOBOTS.
BRING IT, OR THE CRITIC DIES. SEE YOU
THEN.

-NIEMAND KOMPT.

Kompt, whoever he was, had gotten it wrong. At the moment, Halycon Sage did not care if Basel Vasselschnauzer vanished from the face of the earth. But *Ruby!* What was the matter with Stupid? Why hadn't he taken better care of her? Of course she was stubborn, a stubborn woman. If she got some idea in her head there would be no holding her, not even for a horse.

Almost stumbling in his haste, Sage disentangled himself from his computer chair, his fringed leather jacket, and the little drift of possessions that surrounded him—all he owned—and made for the Dirty Dog. Preisczech had described the place in excruciating detail. It seemed to mean something to him, so perhaps he had gone back there, or perhaps the Boys would know something.

Halycon Sage was sure that Preisczech would hand over the whistle if he could be found. They were friends, after all. He had saved Preisczech's life, and this was an emergency. The Vlasco Building, tallest edifice in the nearest large city, was known to all. He cleared his mind, offered up (again) his journey and his quest, and headed out the door.

No-NAME STUPID DID not like fear. Nobody does, of course, but Stupid was more than usually reluctant to feel this emotion, or to admit it when he did. He knew himself susceptible to boredom, disinterest, joy, and a colt-like exhilaration when inspired. He knew that he sometimes looked down on others, was sometimes a little arrogant. But he would not admit to fear.

So at this moment, he thought himself "a little nervous." Ruby had gone, and Halycon Sage had not come back. This was not like either of them. A motel room is really no place for a horse, though he had learned to tolerate it.

The door was closed. He pushed against it with his nose, against the crack of the door, against the doorknob. He could not budge it. He was hungry, and beginning to panic. Suddenly the door burst open. A stout young woman screamed and reeled backward, colliding with her cleaning cart, and No-Name Stupid was on the run again.

CHAPTER
TWENTY

Y SOME HIDDEN law of attraction, everybody was converging on the Dirty Dog. The hidden fate that draws us together and prepares our proper endings was at work. And the end was drawing near.

We should change the name of this bar, though Buzzard, perhaps affected by the presence of the Iraqi family beside him in the booth. They were all back from the mansion for a visit. Abdurraheem looked considerably cheered up. *It don't sound like no place for a kid. It's a great place, deserves a better name*, continued Buzzard's train of thought. *And* dogs *deserve better, too. They're a* wonderful *animal!*

Maybe the Canis Fidelis. the Faithful Dog. This was the title of the only Latin story Buzzard had actually studied at boarding school. *The Canis Fidelis.* Though they had sat through a whole year of class, nobody had learned any Latin. You couldn't, even if you wanted to. Everybody was too busy throwing giant spitballs at the teacher.

The bar was certainly crowded on this beautiful summer morning. The door was open, and the breeze came in. Snake Eyes, Skull, and Bill the Bartender were there. The whole gang was there except Ruby. Wolf was still hanging with Ratbone over by the jukebox. Buzzard, Abdurraheem, Layla, and Nuri were there, all drinking lemonade. A couple of other Mofos had come in to find out what had happened to their leader. Preisczech and Jenny were gone, but had said they would be back. The outside was a parking lot of cars old and battered and cars suspiciously new. There was plenty of transportation, anyway.

There was no sign of Basel Vasselschnauzer. Apparently he had escaped from his loosely tied bonds. Nobody missed him.

There was an expectation in the air, a feeling of waiting. Though the day was fair, it felt like the time before a storm. Streaming sunlight and fresh western air flowed through the open door. Supertramp's "Take the Long Way Home" was playing on the jukebox. Something was going to happen, everyone could feel it.

And it did.

Through the open door came a tall man, well proportioned. He wore a fringed jacket, jeans, and a battered hat. His long black hair was tied back in a ponytail. A few bits of beading and turquoise adorned his person—nothing flashy. He looked tired, and his face was kind.

"Hi, I'm Halycon Sage," said the man.

"Not the great, amazing *Halycon Sage?*" asked Wolf mockingly. He had had a bellyful of Halycon Sage years ago from hearing Ruby yammering on about him. "Surely our little bar could not be so *honored.*"

Sage gave him a look.

"Has anybody seen Preisczech? Eastern European guy, genius scientist, kind of crazy?"

"You don't need to describe him, my man, we know him well," said Ratbone expansively. It was amusing to note that both Ratbone and Basel Vasselschnauzer addressed people as "my man," though with quite different inflections. "Have a drink on us."

Sage agreed with thanks and requested a beer. Saying no, he realized, would alienate these guys, hurt their pride, and trigger a long discussion about *why* he wouldn't drink with them. He didn't have the time.

"Preisczech," he said again after taking a sip of foam.

"Preisczech, alias Lazlo Exlax, alias Buddy Flintstone, alias many more, is currently in love," said Buzzard, rising from the red leather booth. "Therefore there is no knowing his whereabouts."

"That doesn't sound like Preisczech," said Halycon Sage doubtfully.

"Exactly!" replied Buzzard, "which will make his behavior all the more unpredictable."

Beaner didn't know what had gotten into Buzzard lately. Just because you have money is no reason to talk funny.

Halycon Sage thought he had better spill the whole thing quickly, in simple terms. Time was passing.

"Preisczech has a fake cigar box full of these things called nanobots. They're little robots, so small you can't see them, and Preisczech programmed them to take apart all the machines in the world, starting with the nuclear ones, right down to your watch. They can do it, too, because everything they take apart, they use to make more nanobots. And the new ones start doing the same thing.

"So *that's* what that box—"

"Shut up! Listen!"

"The only thing that can stop them," Sage continued, "is this tin whistle he wears around his neck."

"I seen that!" cried Snake Eyes, excited to hear about something he recognized. "But he don't got it no more. He give it to Jenny."

Sage turned a couple of shades of pale.

"It's okay, Preisczech said they'd be right back," Wolf said reassuringly.

"Yeah, but they're in *love*," said Buzzard. "So, their minds are not right, and we can't count on anything they say. They could walk out for cigarettes and send us a postcard from Barbados."

Buzzard was an astute man, though he was way off about the couple's location.

"Gentlemen," came a voice from the door, "allow me to introduce somebody. Is Mrs. Preisczech."

Congratulations, with varying degrees of loudness and physical contact, were offered by all.

"There you *go,*" said Buzzard gesturing with his arm, pleased that his prediction had been partially fulfilled.

"Ma'am," said Sage politely. Then he turned to his friend. "Preisczech. Some maniac has Ruby. And he's got Vasselschnauzer, too. He wants to trade for your whistle, or he's going to kill them. Have you still got your whistle?"

"Still got whistle," said Preisczech. Of course they still had it.

"Still around the neck?" asked Sage.

"Around the neck," confirmed Preisczech. It was, of course, around *Jenny's* neck, but there seemed no reason to mention this.

"Let's go, then," said Sage. "The Vlasco Building, 11:31 tonight. We can talk on the way."

"I want to go too!" yelled Snake Eyes.

"Me too!" shouted Wolf and a couple of others. Even Abdurraheem came forward. The excitement of the chase was on them all. Layla reluctantly followed him, leading Nuri.

"Come on, we'll take the limo," said Rathbone quietly to Halycon Sage. If all this stuff about Preisczech's tiny robots was true, perhaps the end of the world was at hand. Then they wouldn't have to take back the car.

CHAPTER
TWENTY-ONE

THERE WAS NO trace of Halycon Sage at the sandy place by the sparkling stream. No-Name Stupid had run a little distance in his panic, then walked for miles and miles. After checking the stream, he'd been walking around all day, having nowhere else to go. Maybe it had been *more* than one day. He remembered no barn, no pasture, only Ruby and Halycon Sage, and they were gone.

A little while after nightfall, something came toward him. A woman. In his increasing misery he was not paying much attention. Swirling colors, shawls and scarves.

"No-Name Stupid," she said calmly. Her voice was friendly and slightly accented. "Come with me. I will feed and brush you, and give you water. Then we will wait until the time is right. You have a job to do. It is not pleasant, but it is necessary, and it is yours to do. You will not mind it."

Stupid put his nose into her hand—his brown-and-white nose, pink-nostrilled, slightly damp and soft as velvet. He found a bit of apple.

THE VLASCO BUILDING, a high-end office building with a few luxury suites on top, was 13 stories high, quite a skyscraper for a southwestern city. Something of an anomaly, really, and some called it an "eyesore." There was a roof garden on top, and a helipad, complete with waiting helicopter.

Niemand Kompt, Ruby, and Basel Vasselschnauzer also waited, well concealed. Vasselschnauzer complained bitterly that his nose would sunburn. It was getting late and all three were nervous.

There was no talking amongst them. Sometimes enemies talk to pass the time when they are thrown together, finding comfort in their mutual observations and attitudes and the stories of their lives. There was none of that here. Vasselschnauzer was terribly unpleasant in one way and Niemand Kompt in quite another. Ruby, as always, was a woman of few words.

At 11:31, the elevator door opened. Quite a crowd came through: everyone who had set out from the bar along with some curiosity seekers.

"Stay back," said Halycon Sage, apparently quite calm. "This doesn't look too good." He stepped deliberately out into the open, walking around the edges of the roof garden above the thirteenth floor.

"Ruby?" called Halycon Sage, "Can you hear me?"

It happened so fast. From the east side of the garden, behind a group of palm trees, stepped Sean Raintree. From the west (an azalea grove), stepped Lydia Wentworth-Brewster. From the south and north (rock garden and sunflower plantation respectively) came Abu Mu'awiya of al-Qaeda, glad to be out of his damp cave at last, and Lev

Goldstein of Mossad, whom we may not have time to know. For as we have said, the end is near.

It will never be known whether the four were working together or whether the whole thing was the most monstrous coincidence. Surely they would have seen each other, challenged each other, maybe even shot each other, wouldn't they? Wouldn't they? But it hadn't happened like that.

Four guns of different makes and models pointed at the brain and heart of Halycon Sage. Four shots rang out. It will never be known who was the actual killer. Though the nanobots had been busy in their downward progression from most to least dangerous inventions, they had not yet reached the handgun.

Halycon Sage did not fall where he stood. Strangely, inexplicably, his body sailed, almost flew, over the edge of the tall, tall building. Weightless, like a bird in flight. For one moment he was silhouetted against the sky, so graceful, like a forgotten dream. Then, with a flash of turquoise and silver, he was gone.

THE END

Or maybe not . . .

CHAPTER
TWENTY-TWO

HALYCON **S**AGE **DROPPED** the pen and notebook, shaking out his fingers. He was developing writer's cramp trying to get something done while waiting for the kidnapper to show up, and this waiting was getting on his nerves. Never, never had he written anything so long. He was getting the hang of it, though. It would make a nice ending for his autobiography, should he ever really write one. And if anyone reading this might wonder how Sage, a mere author, knew the actual names and identities of the four crack agents who were on his trail . . . well, he *was* the mysterious Halycon Sage. And he had been surfing the Web.

"No, no, nothing yet, sit down," he signaled to Preisczech and Jenny, who sat in another corner of the rooftop garden. The rest of the crowd had been persuaded to wait downstairs on the grounds of safety, both the victims' and their own. The newlyweds were enjoying the garden, murmuring to each other in low tones. Love can make a honeymoon anywhere. But Halycon Sage thought that it just wasn't right. If stupid kidnappers were going to insist on their contacts being so damned punctual, they could at least be on time themselves.

CHAPTER
TWENTY-THREE

OUT OF THE shadows, a cold voice spoke. "Do you have the whistle?"

"Do you have Ruby?" countered Sage.

"You mean Vasselschnauzer," corrected Niemand Kompt.

"*Blank* Vasselschnauzer," said Halycon Sage, using a bad word. "Where's Ruby? No Ruby, no whistle."

"Whistle first," said the cold, cold voice.

This was becoming absurd.

"Come out where I can see you," said Niemand Kompt.

"*Oh,* no. I just did that, and look how it turned out," said Halycon Sage, who sometimes confused his writings with reality.

Niemand Kompt could make nothing of this. There was silence. "Send out Preisczech, then," said the kidnapper. "I want that whistle!"

"Mmmff, mmmf, mfff," said Basel Vasselschnauzer, who was tied and gagged again. The only thing Niemand Kompt had in common with normal people was that he could not stand listening to Basel Vasselschnauzer.

Ruby was tied up too, but much more loosely, for she had been much less annoying. She had made a point of being silent and passive, seeming like no threat, a negligible piece of prettiness, perhaps some inefficient secretary dressed in dusty boots for her day off. Niemand Kompt, essentially a man of emotion, had tied his captives according to their effect on him, and he had counted her no threat. They lay behind him in the shadowed garden—his attention was all for Halycon Sage. And Ruby had managed to wriggle free.

In some ways, Ruby was the exact opposite of Halycon Sage. Sage lived in his dreams, and his reality was fluid. This meant the Divine could come to him, but he could also make mistakes. Ruby saw the world around her and missed nothing.

Ruby had counted on the kidnapper's being too occupied with Sage and Preisczech's whistle to pay any attention to Basel Vasselschnauzer, and she was right. Her plan was this: While he was thus diverted, she intended to tie the rope—the original one, still wound around the critic's waist—securely to one of the decorative pillars near the edge of the garden. (For Niemand Kompt was mad and had not searched either of his captives.) She would lower Basel Vasselschnauzer down one story. It was only a matter of about twenty feet, and the rope was strong and well made. Beneath that part of the garden was an open balcony with French doors that led into one of the luxury suites near the top of the building. Vasselschnauzer could swing himself onto the balcony, avoiding the longer drop to the ground.

Crawling on her belly, she made her way to Basel Vasselschnauzer. Silently she untied him. Ruby was good at things. Like Halycon Sage, she could move without a sound.

She could tie sailors' knots and untie them. She knew karate and other useful arts.

"Get the rope," she breathed to Vasselschnauzer.

"What rope? This?" asked the critic, indicating the cheap, flimsy rope that had held him.

"No, Katzenpauzer, the one you brought with you. Under your shirt."

"I think I dropped it," said Basel Vasselschnauzer. Perhaps, like Halycon Sage, he was good with words, but not very good at real life. They were trapped.

It was a good thing Stupid was used to walking into motel rooms, because he did not mind walking into the elevator, though it was rather small for him. His new friend, the Romany woman, stepped in too. She pushed a golden button. There was an interval of odd, motionless motion. She waited, finger poised. In a few minutes she would push "open," and No-Name Stupid, brown and white pinto and the Pride of Halycon Sage, would step out and save the world.

WHILE ALL THIS was going on, the pointless negotiations continued. "Send out Preisczech," demanded Niemand Kompt.

"Shan't!" said Halycon Sage, reverting to some childhood book from England. His mind was full of odd bits like this, and it seemed an appropriate response.

Kompt was finding Halycon Sage a tough row to hoe. He didn't react like other people.

"Your books stink!" shouted Niemand Kompt, also reverting to childhood.

"Yeah, what clued you in?" asked Sage sarcastically.

This might have gone on forever but for Jenny, who decided that enough was enough. It was her wedding night, and this was not how she had hoped to spend it. Also, her Alex was looking tired, and she intended to care for him as a good wife should. She would not allow him to make himself sick over some stupid whistle, doubtless a relic of his childhood. Why the other man wanted it was incomprehensible, but she had seen men go mad over comic books and action figures and similar things, so this was no surprise.

"Is this what you're looking for?" asked Jenny, stepping forward politely, removing the whistle from her neck. She held it out to Niemand Kompt.

"No!" wailed Preisczech.

"No!" cried Halycon Sage.

Niemand Kompt savored his moment of triumph, holding in his hand more earthly power than anyone had ever known. More than Alexander the Great or Caesar, more than Shaka Zulu or Genghis Khan. More than any president or general. For one moment, Niemand Kompt, apostle of pretension and perverse despair, scorner of ethics and morals—and of kindness—upholder of pointless products and celebrity drivel as the be-all and end-all of existence, held all the power in the world.

And then No-Name Stupid walked out of the elevator, straight over to Niemand Kompt. With one push from his brown and white nose, he nudged the nihilist writer over the side of the building.

It was a long way down.

CHAPTER
TWENTY-FOUR

**O THE DISAPPOINTMENT** of many, the fire department arrived in time. Someone had reported unusual noises on the roof, and a jumper was suspected. There was no jumper—merely a horsenose victim—but the firemen served their purpose. An enormous billowing thing was employed to catch the falling Kompt, like one of those blow-up castles at children's parties but more serious in its coloration and intent. The police, not yet overwhelmed by the failure of every piece of technology in the world (though that was coming soon), questioned witnesses and led Niemand Kompt away in handcuffs.

A few minutes later, a vociferously protesting Basel Vasselschnauzer was also hauled away, proclaiming to anyone who would listen that he needed CAVIAR ON TOAST with lemon, chopped onion, and chopped egg *IMMEDIATELY*; that the whole thing was RIDICULOUS as he was COMPLETELY UNHURT; that the press should ONLY PHOTOGRAPH his GOOD SIDE, and that the covering of the stretcher beneath him would DAMAGE his SKIN with its UNBEARABLE ROUGHNESS. Everyone else on the roof had sworn he was injured just to get rid of him—and it had worked.

The rest of the audience was clearing out, obliviously texting on their soon-to-be-destroyed cell phones. Jenny and Preisczech wanted to go home, and most of the regulars wanted to get back to the bar. They drifted off in twos and threes, laughing and cheering.

It had been a big day. Only Halycon Sage, Ruby, Buzzard, and Abdurraheem remained. Layla and Nuri were tired, and Rathbone had taken them home in the limousine.

"Can you fly one of these things?" Buzzard asked Abdurraheem, walking over to the helipad.

"Sure," he replied. He had trained like mad and could fly anything.

"Like to take a spin?" inquired Buzzard casually. "Mr. Sage?"

"Anthony, you just got me a wonderful *job, alhamdulillah.* I'm not going to steal a *helicopter*!" said Abdurraheem.

"Wouldn't be stealing. It belongs to my mother," said Buzzard, a little shame-faced at his ridiculous level of privilege. "It will fit the four of us."

The Iraqi turned to Halycon Sage. "Do you trust me?" he asked. Oh, to fly again—just once!

Halycon Sage looked into the dark, brilliant, glittering eyes of Muhammad Abdurraheem Hussein, who wore an expression that security officials had sometimes described as "crazed."

"Sure," said Halycon Sage.

CHAPTER
TWENTY-FIVE

REISCZECH HAD THOUGHT long and hard when he programmed the nanobots. Some of his effects were rather eccentric. Electricity still worked, mostly; hospital equipment still worked, but your watch didn't. People were getting good at telling time by the sun again. Luckily there was plenty of that here in the southwest. God only knew what they were doing up in Seattle.

It was a good thing the state had finally invested in solar, wind, and geothermal power, because most of those things still worked. It was also good that, after the economic crash, so many people had started growing gardens and raising chickens. Abdurraheem had shared his awesome gardening skills, leavened with a newly acquired knowledge of organics, and now, in August, everyone was canning frantically, putting up their fruits and vegetables. With a little adaptation, stoves still worked, both gas and electric. Jenny turned out to know all about canning and cooking, and she was teaching others. (Her name had not really been Jenny, of course, but now it was.)

Skull's girlfriend was very proud of her new culinary accomplishments and had found a special cutting board that she marked with "S" on one side for Sweet and "S" on the other for Savory so she wouldn't mix up the sides and make garlic cookies.[1]

The long-distance food distribution system dependent on trucking was dead as a mackerel, and even more serious was the problem of water. But Preisczech was on the case, assisted by Josh, Trevor, and a team of eccentrics that had wandered down out of the mountains, their antiquated skills and futuristic talents needed at last. There was no more hard alcohol, but some of the Boys had set up a still for when conditions improved. Some people *were* learning to make beer. It was really bad beer.

Television didn't work and the demise of the internet had been earth-shattering for many. Trevor had thought he would go mad until, just by chance, he had wandered outside at night and seen the desert stars—really seen them for the first time. Since electricity could only be used for really important things, the ambient light was way down. Without light pollution, the view of the galaxy was breathtaking.

Strangely, reel-to-reel movies still worked. The little town had one theatre, and everyone young and old gathered there on Saturday nights. Ah, Preisczech.

A lot of people were happier now. They walked and rode bicycles more, and ate less and more healthily. They were getting to know each other again, and a truce had been

---

1. For the record, this character's name is Emma, her boyfriend is a jerk, and there are good reasons for her mistake, which she explains in Book Two, *The Book of Squidly Light*

declared in the perennial Western war between the rednecks and the hippies. Punkers, emos, yuppies, Tea Partiers and the other groups were also included. There was simply no time for all that. There was simply no time for all that.

People were no longer "consumers," a word that had been grinding Halycon Sage's gears for many years. They were people again. Advertising was dead, unless you painted your own sign. And paint wasn't thick on the ground, either. (That means there wasn't a lot of it.)

It was hard to know what was happening in far away cities, but this was how things were going in this one small town. Bits of grass and flowers were coming up through the unused freeways, and a few crazy people liked to sunbathe on them. Horses were happier too. They were back at the center of life instead of being expensive luxuries possibly destined for dogfood.

When No-Name Stupid was not needed for riding or hauling, he roved all day, always returning for supper. Both he and Halycon Sage were a lot healthier as junk food was a thing of the past. Halycon Sage did not have to submit any more novels and Rathbone did not have to return the limo. He was still fond of it even though it was no good for driving anymore. It was being used as a greenhouse. Halycon Sage *did* finally finish his autobiography and Ruby sent it by horse post to Kathryn out east, on the off chance that books were still being published.

Thriving businesses had sprung up for weaving cloth, making wagon wheels, and shoeing horses. People remembered that the name "Fletcher" meant "arrow maker," as that trade was in demand again. The demise of guns had been a shock to many in the same way the end of the internet had shocked the young—as an unimaginable change in the most basic assumptions of life. This was the West, after all. But trucks and guns were being replaced by horses, bikes, and arrows. There was simply no other choice. Ruby, already a trick rider, had taught some of the Dogs the basic horsemanship skills, and they were teaching others.

Halycon Sage was in great demand, as he was not only a pretty good rider, but turned out to be expert with a bow and arrow. His shots were so accurate as to be almost painless to his quarry, and he always sent thanks to the animal's spirit in the traditional manner. After all these years, Halycon Sage had finally found something practical he could do. Sometimes he took Whining Deadeye Vasselschnauzer with him, but mostly he preferred to hunt in silence.

Of course all these relationships between humans, animals, plants, and the living planet would have to be readjusted. *Everything* would. But for the End of the World, it was not too bad.

EPILOGUE

EVERYTHING WAS ALL right now at the Dirty Dog Bar, called by some the Canis Fidelis Bar and Grill. There was still the green felt pool table and the big, faded cowboys-on-horses mural covering one wall, while the rest of the walls were sun-bleached ancient wood. But now the open door and the newly cleaned windows let in light and air. There was also one of those beer signs with a moving waterfall, restful and poetic. It shouldn't have worked, as no other technology of comparable sophistication and frivolity was functioning anywhere in the world, but it did. Devout beer drinkers attributed this to a miracle.

"What happened to the whistle, Uncle Bill?" asked Nuri, who was helping make lemonade at a long table. "The one that controlled the tiny robots." He never tired of hearing how the world had changed so suddenly and the great part they had all played in it. Sometimes, like now, he thought of a new question to ask.

"It fell out of that guy's hand when he flew off the building," said Ratbone, stepping up to the bar. "Fell into my old friend, the trash compactor."

"The one we crashed the limo into when Deadeye was goin' crazy in the back," put in Wolf.

"We didn't crash, we glided gently to a halt," amended Ratbone. "But yeah, same truck, same driver. Don't hardly seem possible a guy could be so many places at once. Anyway, that whistle was squashed flat. We done looked. Don't work no more."

"Moosehead . . . Mossad. Moosehead . . . Mossad," mumbled Lev Goldstein to himself on the other side of the bar. The new moosehead was being installed, and these simple things are amusing when one is speaking a foreign language.

Lev Goldstein was stuck here for good. Planes didn't work. Cars didn't work. Only horses and bicycles still worked. Abu Mu'awiya was stuck here as well, glad to be out of Al-Qaeda and his soggy cave in the otherwise dry mountains. The two had definitely not made friends, but they had started comparing notes. They had a lot in common. Both were highly trained in similar specialties. Both were sick of war and politics, and neither had any way to get home.

"I wonder how everyone is doing over there," said Abu Mu'awiya. "God willing they're okay."

"God willing," said Lev Goldstein with a sigh.

The Dirty Dog Bar had always had a strange subterranean goodness, entirely at odds with its name and surface appearance. Now it was a hub of community activity, a locus of eating, planning, relaxing, and general hanging out for all the oddly assorted characters of the new civilization. Sunlight streamed in, gilding the marmalade fur of the cat sprawled across Abdurraheem's lap. For, strangely, the end of air pollution had also spelled the end of his allergies. The cat purred loudly and rhythmically, and the people at the table smiled at each other.

The amount of sweetness and light around here is getting sickening, thought Skull. He missed the smoke and darkness of the old days, and the unidentifiable scum on the tables. *Wish I could move across town, start a* real *bar,* he thought.

In contrast, Halycon Sage was entirely happy with the new establishment. He felt comfortable inviting his friends there. And as fragments of his past life continued to float back into his consciousness, one more mystery had been explained: his firm conviction that a *real* bar required a moosehead. For it turned out that the earliest of his patchy, distant memories showed himself, six years old, sitting with his father in a bar under a similar trophy on a golden afternoon, deep in the Nevada desert.

He gently shook away the memory, turning from reverie to the demands of present hospitality. "It's alright, you can come in," called Halycon Sage, leaning halfway out the door. "We've got a moosehead now."

THE END

AFTERWORD

WHILE ALMOST EVERY person in this novel is made up, many of the incidents actually happened, and some of the places are real. "The Hangman—Lousy Food, Warm Beer," was real, as was their old wooden sign which I sometimes rode past as a child. (And by the way, I do not take the issue of Indian alcoholism lightly! Alcohol was such a pervasive part of my background that it simply could not be filtered out.)

The heavenly smell of sage after rain and the mysteriously vanished tumbleweeds are also real—cheers to those who love or remember these things! Like my protagonist, I hacked through a forest of compacted tumbleweeds, escaped from a waterlogged tent to a chain coffee shop during a news-making storm in Klamath Falls, and was the most minor and forgettable of writers, trying to save the world by the same unsuccessful methods Halycon Sage himself originally employed.

Real people in the novel:

- Larry Cloud Morgan, who appears as himself. The stories about him are true, and my interactions with him were as described.

- A Native American elder, here unnamed, who conferred a silent blessing was also real.

- Literary critic Hamden McPete, that small, urbane and deeply courteous man, raising a glass of the best alcohol and speaking in a rolling baritone, is modeled closely on Dr. Robert Gorrell, professor of Shakespeare studies, one-time university president, and husband of my mother in her final years. He moved the book from seven words, two sentences and a footnote to a quarter page of minor wit by writing me that it "might be a caprice, a whimsy, or even a lowland fling, but [was] definitely *not* a novel." And thanks to Pat Melange for saying, "*Some kind of ho, anyway.*"

- The Miplisser Rebbe is based on a real person from Minneapolis (Mpls).

- Most people believe the kind adviser who tied up his horse next to Sage's was real.

- Officer Sunshine, though I can find nothing about him on the internet, was reputed to be real in the 1970's.

The Life and Times of Halycon Sage, now *The Way Beyond*, began for me just as it did for the protagonist. I awakened with the words, "One-hundred-and-one cows: a novel," echoing mysteriously in my mind. Most of the book came easily, the second half in a period of two days after the manuscript had spent several years in a file drawer. Almost from the beginning, the characters took on a life of their own and told me things I didn't know. I had no idea how Ratbone got his name or why Halycon Sage refused to answer interview questions until these things appeared in the course of the story. And the reason for his obsession with mooseheads, also from real life, was revealed last of all.

This book was begun in a period between the passing of my spiritual teacher and my return to what Hesse called "the golden track," so Sage's encounter with the Wise Being is somewhat ambiguous and bittersweet—my encounters with non-ordinary reality have been neither!

APPENDIX
SOPHIE'S TERM PAPER

THE FOLLOWING PAPER is one of the many, many analyses of the works of Halycon Sage, found everywhere from high school and even middle school classes to the highest reaches of academic writing and literary criticism. This sample draft from a young person, though obviously faulty, shows promise. We include her teacher's comments in the belief that they throw a modest yet beneficial light on the development of one emerging scholar in the field of Halycon Sage Criticism as she elucidates the issues that preoccupy its practitioners, proponents, and detractors.

Note: Worthy as this essay doubtless is, comprising some 30 pages in its entirety, space considerations prevent us from offering more than a brief sample. But we hope it is enough to convince any skeptical reader that it is indeed possible for hundreds of thousands of words to have been written on the seemingly short and simple works of Halycon Sage.

—The Editors

Analysis and Criticism of a Modern Novel

Major Themes in 101 Cows: A Novel - First Draft

Sophie McGregor

AP Modern Literature, Dry Creek Gulch High School

Professor Catwell

May 23, 20

"In fact, the creative invention is so dense that an adequate commentary on the book would be longer than the book itself." –Colin Wilson[1]

There may be those among the *uninformed public* who question *why* and even *how* numerous treatises, papers, chapters, scholarly and popular articles and even entire *books* have been written analyzing and parsing the extremely brief and terse works of Halycon Sage.

"Wonder" would be better than "question" here.

There is no need to resort to italics in the first paragraphs of your essay. I have taught you better than that!

How can such short works give birth to such voluminous fountains of theory, conclusion and speculation? But of course this is the whole genius of the post-modernist minimalist neo-symbolist pseudo-realist school of which the revered Mr. Sage is the unchallenged and universally acknowledged founder.

"Sage is a true artist, and his genius is his embrace of the minimalist tradition. Sage is the standard bearer for all that is simple, clean, clear, and yet complex. One word of Sage's is worth a thousand words of lesser authors," writes noted critic Basel Vasselschnauzer.[2] Dr. Vasselschnauzer[3] is spot on, except that, far from merely *embracing* the minimalist tradition, Sage is its undisputed founder. Even the many pieces written on *One Hundred and One Cows* have not succeeded in plumping its depths.

In order to extract some of the flavor, meaning, and essence of this extraordinary novel by this unique and unparalleled 21st Century writer, it is first necessary to examine the novel itself, phrase by phrase and sometimes even word by word.

The novel is reproduced in full here and will be broken down in the subsequent sections to address the many fascinating issues raised by it's different components.

(We will deal with the Author's Note in a separate section.)

One Hundred and One Cows: A Novel

By Halycon Sage

There are no cows in this book. What there is, however, is the story of Rory McPhooey, who sailed from the fogbound coasts of Ireland all by himself in a tiny, tiny boat, all the way to the shores of the Native Americans, who turned him right back around and sent him home again.

The End.

The novel in its entirety brings up many fascinating issues, not least the matter of what kind of boat the daring explorer McPhooey utilized, where he got it, how he paid for it, and how, being of extremely small size as is attested in the novel, it was seaworthy enough to navigate the entire Atlantic Ocean not once but twice. And whether he returned safely. And how he was received if and when he did. And whether his almost momentary visit left any mark on the Native American tribes

The infectious enthusiasm you demonstrate here, though obviously
not appropriate for an academic paper, bodes well for your valedictorian speech!

who were in contact with him. Whether, for instance, any

Irish customs or cultural vestiges can be identified in the

relics of Atlantic costal tribes.

You are
rather too fond of
the word "fascinating".

But all this is a digression, though a fascinating one. Time

and paper are limited, and the temptation to dig ever deeper

into the twists and turns of this intriguing subject must be

resisted. Therefore, let us return to our muttons!   What??

What on earth have you been reading? You must be kidding! "Return to our muttons"?
No one has used this expression since about 1920, and even then it was stilted,
antiquated, rare and peculiar!   You're my star pupil, Sophie –
                                                         get a grip!

I.   The Title

"One Hundred and One Cows: A Novel." The first thing

that leaps to the eye of the attentive reader is the number

cliché

One Hundred and One (101). This caused great excitement

in the Arab and Muslim worlds as certain scholars[4]

maintained that, as 101 is the number of prayer beads

on the Muslim rosary, the novel should be subjected to

Islamic scholarship. Their view is confirmed, they say,

by the immediate mention of *cows*, surely a reference to

Chapter 2 of the Qur'an ("The Cows").

These theorists were immediately attacked from opposite

sides, as both puritan-fundamentalists and secular

modernists chimed in, maintaining that Sage's title could not *possibly* refer to prayer beads as no person of good morals or good sense used them anymore, their use being (variously) a shocking pagan-derived heresy or a silly old superstition. The scholarly debate, particularly in Great Britain, descended to a level which culminated with the comment "Shut yer gob!"[5] at which point serious students of literary criticism ceased to follow it.

A more romantic element (see Edward Said's *Orientalism*) maintained that, since a great part of Sage's strategy appears to be making his novels as short as possible, the number 101 is really a coded reference to 1001, or *One Thousand and One Nights* (in English, *The Arabian Nights*), and should thus be interpreted solely in the light of that classic imaginative work. Jewish scholars countered that 101 is really the binary number 5 which represents the five levels of the soul in *Kabbalah*, as interpreted by the Miplisser Rebbe.[6] Alternately, 5 is the gematria (numerological value) of the Hebrew letter "Hay" a common abbreviation for the unpronounceable name of God. And since cows eat *hay*, the Great Sage was also making a veiled reference to the "spark of holiness" within all living things.

Other commentators leave the number aside and focus solely on the mention of cows, accounting for it in different ways according to their individual interests: Physiological, psychological, sociological, philosophical, linguistic or metaphysical. These analyses, while fascinating, are beyond the scope of this paper. *Last sentence unnecessary!*

I. The Text

"There are no cows in this book." What a surprise, what a shock, what a stunning reversal of expectations! Could any but the most innovative and daring writer state immediately that *there are no cows* when the very title, the very fulcrum and guidepost of the novel's purported subject, is (are) cows? Does the absence of cows imply the absence of nourishment (e.g., milk), and thus of love? Does it imply the absence of meaning, of substance, of reality itself?[7] Is this thus a work of existentialism? Or of solipsism? Or even of nihilism? Is Halycon Sage secretly no better than Niemand Kompt?[8] Or is he truly a harbinger of The New Sanity?[9] Again, a full analysis of these fascinating issues is beyond our scope here, but the endnotes should point the interested reader in the right direction.

"This thus" will have an odd "tick-tock" sound to readers who pronounce the words aloud in their heads and they are not a few. Rephrase.

Sophie!

FYI, a good writer wields the written word with a dexterity which renders the use of italics for emphasis unnecessary.

167

Moving on to my next set of considerations . . .

[Excerpt ends here. Corresponding footnotes are included below for clarity. Be sure to examine them carefully, as they are integral to understanding the main text. At the end are the teacher's final comments. The Editors]

Notes

1. Colin Wilson in the Introduction to David Lindsay's *The Violet Apple,* (add date & publisher)

2. "What We Like and Why," *New York Times-Enquirer,* May 26, 20

3. We, the author of this essay, are giving Dr. Vasselschnauser this courtesy title since he has always maintained that he has a Ph.D., despite the difficulties cited by certain cynical persons in identifying its exact date and origin. The allegations concerning "Chickappee Online University" have never been substantiated.

4. Rauf Habib Rauf, Ph.D., Abdulwali Makram, Ph.D., Marvin Marvins, D.D.S. (Cite articles.)

5. "Religious Symbolism behind *101 Cows? Hogwash!*" The Daily Yell, February , 20

6. "Did Halycon Sage Channel the Miplisser Rebbe?" by Morris Ayin, Jewish *Daily Backward,* April 20 .

7.   See Chapter 26, "Why Do I See Nothing?"
in Atherton Grump's monumental work, *Is Life
Meaningless?*

8.   E.g. fiction: *The Black Gray Dark, Decay, The
Swamp of Despair, Nothing,* and *Suzie Goes to the
Races (and Dies),* and nonfiction: *Filling the Void
with Talk Shows* and *I'm Fabulous, You're a Necrotic
Collection of Worm-Food.* Also *We Grasp at Straws
and the Water Tears Them Loose.*

9.   *Toward a New Sanity: Finding Light
Everywhere,* Amrit Patel, Marvin Rosenbaum and
Ali Halim, 20██. Also *Letting in the Air, Love is
Stronger* and *Wake Up, Dumbass, You Need to Save
the Planet!* (add authors and citations).
Your citations are somewhat irregular
  (and obviously incomplete in this first draft).
  Please use APA Style.
   In General: Good job, Sophie! Good job!

GLOSSARY

Advaita–nonduality, from Hinduism

Alhamdulillah–"All praise to God", "the praise is to God". This common phrase implies that anyone who is praising or admiring anything is really praising the One Source of the attractive qualities which they admire

Boo Radley–a reclusive character in *To Kill a Mockingbird*

Burka–a head-to-toe covering worn by a small minority of Muslim women

Dharma–the Wheel of the (Natural) Law, the natural and proper order of things, good and right conduct and organization of society

Dua–a spontaneous, sincere personal prayer from the heart

Grok, grokked–a Martian language word meaning to understand deeply, literally "to drink." From Robert Heinlein's *Stranger in a Strange Land*

Lipstick–that red stuff you put on your lips

Majratan–a Somali tribal group

Mofo–Originally a Not Very Nice Word, for many it has come to mean, like several such words, simply "a guy"

Moschiach–the Jewish Messiah

Mu'awiya–Look it up, we haven't got time

Ogaden–a Somali group whose core territory now lies within Ethiopian borders

Om Namo Bhagavate Vasudevaya–a Hindu mantra to the indwelling God

Orange Sunshine–a form of LSD made by Nicholas Sand and Tim Scully in an underground lab during the 1960's

Tauheed–Unity, from Islam

Yusuf, Maryam, and Issa–the Arabic names for Joseph, Mary, and Jesus

Thor the Dentist–A new comic book character, appearing here for the first time

INDEX
THE WORKS OF HALYCON SAGE
(In Order of Appearance by Page Number)

APPRECIATIONS

EARTFELT THANKS TO Rabbi Yonassan Gershom, Chandi Lyn, and B.C. Hatch, the editors who've worked so hard on various editions of this book; to longtime friend and work-partner Jeneane Harter; to all who have read the manuscript and made suggestions; and to the fascinating groups and unique characters from many cultures who have enriched my life. Without you, this book would not be here.

A loving and appreciative shout-out to my family including John and Garek Bushnell, Elizabeth Vargas-Bushnell-Gunn, Cecily Pinkerton, and a kaleidoscopic menagerie of Vargases, Berliners, Bushnells, and others, including everybody's pets.

Finally, to those who fight for truth against lies (including many of those mentioned above), knowing that both the lies and truth can take many forms. And to cats, parrots, dogs, moose, walruses, and other animals. And to Planet Earth. You're a wonderful planet, and I hope we can arrange to keep you around.

ABOUT THE AUTHOR

MULTICULTURAL BY BIRTH, association, and choice, Karima Vargas Bushnell (M.A. Intercultural Relations) has described herself as "a short, part-Hispanic, Irish-fiddle-playing, Jewish-wisecracking, partly-Black-acculturated Sufi Muslim". Family lore and some research indicate that her great-grandfather was full-blooded Native American.

Though life has taken her north and east and much of her heart remains in the deserts and mountains of the Southwest, she has finally fallen in love with the Upper Midwest where she now lives: with the glorious flowering jungle of summer, the ubiquitous bee and butterfly gardens, the beautiful lakes and nature areas, the orchestra of crickets, cardinals, blue jays, and redwing blackbirds, and most of all the glorious blue heron, a modern flying dinosaur.